The Annihilation of Fish and other stories

Anthony C Winkler

MACMILLAN CARIBBEAN WRITERS

Macmillan Education
Between Towns Road, Oxford, OX4 3PP
A division of Macmillan Publishers Limited
Companies and representatives throughout the world

www.macmillan-caribbean.com

ISBN 1 4050 2639 1

First published 2004

'Absentee Ownership of Cows', 'The Annihilation of Fish', 'Hard Woman', 'New Banana', 'The Thief', 'The Trip to Paris' and 'Unconventionality' all first appeared in the *Jamaica Sunday Observer* between May 2000 and March 2002.
'The Man Who Knew the Price of All Fish' first appeared in 1980 in *Significance: The Struggle We Share* by John H. Brennecke and Robert G. Amick, published by Glencoe Publishing Co. Inc., Encino, California.

Typeset by EXPO Holdings, Malaysia
Cover illustration by Judy Ann Macmillan

Printed and bound in Great Britain

2008 2007 2006 2005 2004
10 9 8 7 6 5 4 3 2 1

Series Preface

Anthony C Winkler has written several of the funniest novels ever to come out of the Caribbean. *The Annihilation of Fish* is his first collection of short stories, and reveals this author's gift is not only for comedy. He writes out of a tolerant understanding of the human condition in general, and a sympathy and love for the Jamaican psyche in particular. His characters are engagingly familiar in their flaws and foibles as they plot murder, commit bribery, burn down churches, hold conversations with the dead, lose their hearts, correspond with a cow, or wrestle with the Devil. These are tales in which the most inconsequential of remarks or incidents can have the most cataclysmic of consequences. Yet in the saddest of stories there still lurks an impish humour and a challenge to the reader to see things differently, to think afresh.

The Macmillan Caribbean Writers Series (MCW) is an exciting new collection of fine Caribbean writing which treats the broad range of the Caribbean experience. As well as short stories and novels the series includes poetry anthologies and collections of plays particularly suitable for Arts and Drama Festivals. There are also works of non-fiction such as an eyewitness account of life under the volatile Soufriere volcano, and another of the removal of an entire village to make way for an American base in World War II.

The series introduces unknown work by newly discovered writers, and in addition showcases new writing and favourite classics by established authors such as Winkler, Michael Anthony, Jan Carew, Ian McDonald and G C H Thomas. Writers on the list come from around the region, including Guyana, Trinidad, Tobago, Barbados, St Vincent, Bequia, Grenada, St Lucia, Dominica, Montserrat, Antigua, the Bahamas, Jamaica and Belize.

MCW was launched in 2003 at the Caribbean's premier literary event, the Calabash Festival in Jamaica. Macmillan Caribbean is also proud to be associated with the work of the Cropper Foundation in Trinidad, developing the talents of the region's most promising emerging writers, many of whom are contributors to MCW.

Judy Stone
Series Editor
Macmillan Caribbean Writers

The Macmillan Caribbean Writers Series

edited by Judy Stone

Novels:

Jeremiah, Devil of the Woods: *Martina Altmann*
Butler, Till the Final Bell: *Michael Anthony*
Such As I Have: *Garfield Ellis*
The Boy from Willow Bend: *Joanne C Hillhouse*
Dancing Nude in the Moonlight: *Joanne C Hillhouse*
Ginger Lily: *Margaret Knight*
Exclusion Zone: *Graeme Knott*
The Humming-Bird Tree: *Ian McDonald*
There's No Place Like ...: *Tessa McWatt*
Ruler in Hiroona: *G C H Thomas*

Plays:

Champions of the Gayelle: (*ed Judy Stone*)
Plays by Alwin Bully, Zeno Constance & Pat Cumper
More Champions of the Gayelle: (*ed Judy Stone*)
Plays by Winston Saunders, Dennis Scott & Godfrey Sealy

Stories:

Going Home, and other tales from Guyana: *Deryck M Bernard*
The Sisters, and Manco's stories: *Jan Carew*
The Annihilation of Fish and other stories: *Anthony C Winkler*

For Gary Buslik

Contents

Preliminary Report	1
The Story of the Fifth Boy	14
Unconventionality	21
A Sign of the Times	29
Absentee Ownership of Cows	34
The Dog	43
The Chance	50
The Interpreter	59
Hard Woman	69
The Big Picture	79
The Cultivator Who Lost His Heart	87
The Riddle	96
New Banana	106
The Man Who Knew the Price of All Fish	114
The Trip to Paris	119
The Thief	125
Dawn Song	134
The New Headmaster	141
The Happy Days of Dog Eat Dog	148
The Annihilation of Fish	156

Preliminary Report

Preliminary Report.
Friday, 15th March, 2002.
District of Ewarton.

Inspector Jordan Hall, in command of my district, has requested a preliminary report on the unusual events of last month concerning an alleged accident between a stake-body truck driven at a high rate of speed, estimated in excess of 50mph in a 35mph zone, by one Emanuel Livingston of the district known as Back-a-Wall, and a tourist who was a pedestrian. Measurements made at the scene of the accident showed skid marks exceeding 700 feet backwards from the point of impact, confirming that the truck was travelling at an unlawful speed. I therefore gave the driver a citation for dangerous driving and also warned him of possible additional charges of reckless endangerment or manslaughter. When he became rowdy and uncooperative, I handcuffed him and placed him under arrest for resisting an officer.

I did not draw my weapon at any time. It is untrue that I pointed it at the driver's friends and threatened to shoot their "rass". Butu will tell lie on him own mother. (I'm aware that Headquarters frowns on the use of "Butu" to indicate a certain lower class of Jamaicans, but this being only a preliminary report, I've taken some liberties with vocabulary. "Butu" will, of course, be edited out of the final report.)

As I was making measurements and taking statements from eyewitnesses, I was approached by a white woman, who identified herself as the victim's friend who had been walking beside him when he was struck. I questioned her on the sequence of events leading up to the accident, and she confirmed eyewitness reports. Her manner, however, seemed strange and not what you would expect from someone whose friend was lying dead on the pavement. For example, when I covered the victim with a body tarp so that gathered onlookers, of whom there were many, would not be afforded the opportunity to gawk at the poor dead man (certainly that could be construed as harassment of a tourist), the woman asked me, "What are you doing? He doesn't like to be wrapped up that way."

"Madam," I pointed out in my official voice, "he's dead."

"What does that mean?"

I thought she was making a joke, albeit in bad taste, so I replied, "He's no more. He's gone."

"Gone!" she exclaimed, pointing. "He's right there!"

I decided the joke had gone far enough. "Madam," I asked respectfully, "what would you like us to do with the body?"

"I have no idea what you're talking about."

"Madam, when people die, they leave a body behind."

"They do?"

My patience, as the superintendent will appreciate, was by now coming to an end.

"Madam, where do you live?"

"Oh, I live right here."

"You nuh live here!" an old lady nicknamed Mad Woman Bellamy interposed without being invited. "No white people live here!"

Mad Woman Bellamy is a known busybody and eccentric who has no family and is said to be the oldest resident in the district. I respectfully requested that she not interfere with an official investigation in progress. I did not say to her, as is alleged, "Hush up you rass mouth! A me in charge." First of all, being a Christian, I do not use such words as "rass". Second of all, I was raised to always show respect to our seniors no matter how interfering and petty and boasty and annoying and cantankerous they might be. Third, and most important, I was in uniform conducting an official inquiry at the scene of an accident and was cognizant that members of the tax-paying public were present – although between you and me, the kind of Butu surrounding me that day don't pay a penny of tax and would thief your chicken quicker than a mongoose.

"Can I wake up my friend and go?" the tourist woman asked. "Today's my birthday."

Nurse Violette Spaulding, who had been summoned to the scene of the accident, the medical officer for the district being abroad doing a course, and who had officially certified that the victim was dead, shook her head sadly. "Your friend is dead, missus," she said gravely.

"But happy birthday, anyhow," I said, trying to cheer her up. "How old are you today?"

The tourist woman replied, "I'm ten millennia old."

Silence now descended over the Butu who, being inquisitive, had encircled us in their desire to eavesdrop on the official police interrogation of this strange white woman.

"Ten millennia?" one man said. "What dat mean?"

You could almost hear Butu brain cells rattling in their brainpan as they did the calculations.

"How much year dat mek?" one Butu asked aloud.

"Shh, me a calculate, man!"

"You trying to tell me, madam", I said, putting Butu out of their calculation misery, "that you're ten thousand years old?"

A gasp went up among the onlookers. Furious whispering and suss-susshing swept over them like a breeze blowing through a woodland.

"That's about right," the witness said. "Now, I'm going to wake up Edward and leave."

Let me pause to make one fact clear. The man was dead. Nurse Spaulding, a medical veteran of over twenty years, had pronounced him dead. I myself, in accordance with our training manual, had applied known government-approved yardsticks for determining death. The gentleman had no heartbeat. He had no pulse. He was not breathing. His eyes were dilated. The reason for all this inactivity? The man lying on the pavement was dead, not half-dead, or three-quarters-dead, but fully dead.

We were therefore unprepared for what happened next.

Before I could restrain her, the tourist woman darted over to the covered body of her dead companion and touched him somewhere on the head, which caused the dead man to kick off the tarp and leap to his feet like a frisky goat, his injuries miraculously gone. Not a scratch was apparent on his body.

Pandemonium and confusion broke out among the onlookers. Screams rent the air. Several women fainted. An elderly gentleman began gasping for breath and had to be attended to by Nurse Spaulding. Butu gaped at the scene with wonder.

"Constable Humphreys," Nurse Spaulding said to me, "wasn't dat man just dead?"

I confirmed that he was.

"Den how come him jump up and walking around?"

I replied that, pending further inquiry, I could not give an official answer to that question.

Butu swarming around us overheard these remarks, which roused them to fever pitch.

I addressed the tourist woman, "Please explain how this dead man came back to life."

The man said something to the woman in a strange tongue that was as mystifying to all hearing it as St Elizabeth patois or schoolboy Latin. She then turned to me as Butu drew closer to listen.

"We don't understand what 'dead' means."

Butu gasped. Mad Woman Bellamy, being a chronic troublemaker, jumped in and bawled, "It mean life stop. You spirit leave you body!"

"But what happens to this?" the man asked above the background babble, indicating with a sweep of his arms his entire physical body.

"Oh, we put it into a hole in the ground," I said, realizing for the first time that perhaps they came from a country with different burying customs.

The woman screamed, and the man said something in his language that sound like "Yuk".

Some in the crowd mimicked his cry of disgust.

"You mean to say", the woman asked, looking incredulous, "that this will happen to all of you? You die and leave your body behind? Then it is put into a hole in the ground? Then what?"

"Then we leave it there," I said quickly, before Mad Woman Bellamy could butt in again.

Again the tourist woman screamed. Many in the crowd, grasping fully for the first time the horror the woman seemed to reflect, also screamed.

At this point, again I forcefully intervened. It is untrue, however, that I threatened to shoot the next member of the public who screamed without permission. At no point did I say, "Butu, stop you bawling or you goin' feel gunshot!"

The two tourists exchanged rapid-fire remarks in their native tongue, the man turning to face Mad Woman Bellamy as if to direct his next question to her.

"Excuse me," I said politely. "I am in charge here. Ask me all your pertinent questions, for only I and I alone can give you an official answer."

"We were wondering", said the man, after exchanging glances with his companion, "why you don't complain to the authorities about this shabby treatment."

"What shabby treatment you a talk 'bout?" Mad Woman Bellamy butted in.

"That all of you must die and have your bodies put into a hole. That's an outrage. You shouldn't put up with it."

"Is de Creator's will, bwoy!" Mad Woman Bellamy scolded him. "A him make de world and we. Him alone decide dat everyone who live must dead! Praise be him name!"

The two tourists became agitated and chattered excitedly with one another.

Finally, the woman said, "We also have a creator."

"What your creator name?" an older man known as Elder McIntyre asked.

"Joe," the man said.

"Joe!" one Butu scoffed. "You saying dat you god name Joe? How can you worship a god name Joe? Wha' kind a fool-fool name dat?"

"Oh," said the tourist woman, "he used to have a longer, more formal name. Something like 'Almighty, most merciful, most bountiful, most all-powerful God', or something like that, wasn't it, Edward?"

Her friend nodded and put in, "Then one day he suddenly said, 'This is too silly. Just call me Joe.'"

"So what you so boasty 'bout wid you god name Joe?" asked Mad Woman Bellamy. "Our god is a good god. He give us eternal life when we dead. But you have to earn it."

"How do you do that?" the tourist man asked mildly.

"You don't thief. You don't lie. You don't covet you neighbour's wife. And you don't take de Lord's name in vain."

"What does that mean?"

"It mean you don't say 'Jesus Christ' like you popping a oath."

"What happens if you do?" asked the tourist woman.

"Well, if you do, and you dead before asking forgiveness, you go straight down to hell." Mad Woman Bellamy pointed to the earth.

"Foolishness!" a rude boy who is a known atheist shouted.

"Hell? What is this hell?" the tourist man wondered.

I answered the tourist man. "Hell is a place of eternal punishment for bad souls. It is a great sea of fire in which wicked souls are burned for eternity."

"You mean," the tourist woman gasped, sounding as if she was losing self-control, "first, you die and leave your body behind to be stuffed into a hole? Then if you said 'Jesus Christ' before you died ..."

"Without begging forgiveness," Mad Woman Bellamy interrupted.

"... your spirit goes to hell where it is burned forever?"

"Burn like firewood!" Mad Woman Bellamy chortled.

The tourist woman fainted. Quickly the man was kneeling at her side, stroking her hair and whispering soothingly to her in their strange tongue.

He scanned the Butu faces that peered down at him and said, "Marguerite always has a bad reaction to injustice. She'll recover in a bit."

"Injustice!" Mad Woman Bellamy shrieked. "Rules are rules. At least we have eternal life. What you have dat's better?"

The crowd pressed forward to hear the white man's answer. The woman revived and got to her feet. She signalled to her companion that she would answer the question.

"Joe gives us eternal life from the start. We don't have to die to get it. We don't have to do anything, pass any test or refrain from saying anything."

A stunned silence greeted this revelation. Then a murmur of wonderment ran through the crowd.

"Him spoil you, den!" Mad Woman Bellamy shrieked. "It come too easy. You don't appreciate what you have!"

"He loves us," the tourist woman replied. "That's why he's so kind to us."

You could have heard a pin drop – although that is not an official remark. One woman, a well-known sensible sister in the district, said, "Our God loves us, too. But he wants us to be strong and tough when we reach heaven."

"Why?" pressed the tourist man. "Isn't your god all-powerful like Joe?"

"Of course!" another sister snapped.

"So why do you need to be strong and tough?"

"Because", Elder McIntyre said, seeing that the women were stumped, "him don't want no sissy in heaven. Him want only strong sheep."

"Is there such a thing as strong sheep?" the tourist woman asked quietly. "Remember, Edward," she said to her companion, "those animals we saw when we visited Bellevue? The ones with the fuzzy coats – those were sheep."

The man laughed at the idea of strong sheep, upsetting the elder.

"Please do not laugh at our Jamaican sheep, sah," Elder McIntyre said in an angry voice, "or I'll bust you head with a stone!"

"Nobody licking any tourist in my jurisdiction," I said firmly. "That would be harassment of a visitor."

It is untrue that I said, "Pick up a stone, and I'll shoot your rass."

Butu is by nature jealous and hate to hear that another man is getting better treatment or enjoying life more, so when they found out that Joe treated his creations better than God treated them, they naturally wanted to lick down somebody or burn down something.

Various Butu in the crowd appealed for calm. One brought up the crucifixion as an example that they were loved by their creator as much as the tourists were by Joe, but when the woman and man heard the whole story in snippets about Mount Calvary and Jesus, the two of them turned whiter, if that was possible.

"You mean this poor man was impaled on a wooden cross because God, his father, was mad at you?"

"Dat's not how I would state the case," said Elder McIntyre huffily.

"So how would you state the case?" the tourist man asked.

Elder McIntyre thought while the crowd fell silent and awaited his wisdom.

"I would say dat God wanted to teach us how to suffer, so he sent down his only begotten son to earth to show us by example."

"But if he loves you," the tourist woman asked impatiently, "why does he want you to suffer?"

Mad Woman Bellamy pushed herself forcefully back into the argument. "De whole story begin wid Adam and Eve in de Garden o' Eden," she said almost angrily. "If dem don't disobey, we in Paradise now and nobody suffer one thing."

"Adam and who?" the tourist man asked.

Onlookers eagerly chipped in pieces of the story of the Fall from Eden. They told about the perfect land where these two aborigines lived, and how the subtle serpent tempted Eve to eat the forbidden fruit – the whole rigmarole that we learn in Sunday school.

When the explanations were finished, the tourist man and woman talked it over in their strange tongue, with many gestures and remarks passing back and forth between them.

Then the man turned to the crowd and said, "John and June."

A strange silence fell over the throng. Finally, Mad Woman Bellamy asked, "Who?"

And the tourist man and woman explained the story of John and June.

Joe, they said, had also begun his creation small, with two prototypes, John and June.

"What name 'prototypes'?" one Butu wondered.

"Experimental models," the tourist man said.

The woman picked up the story. She said that one of the creatures in Paradise with John and June was a strange animal called a brayglock, which made a nasty sound worse than a donkey's braying. And he made it constantly and loudly, much to the annoyance of John and June. One day, quite by accident, John discovered that a good kick to its backside would shut up the creature. But Joe so liked the sound the brayglock made that he told John and June, "Any of my creatures canst thou kick, except the brayglock, whose sound is beloved to me. Him thou must not kicketh."

The tourist man took over. He related that one day John was taking a nap under a tree, when the brayglock, running a joke, snuck up to him and blasted him with its horrible bray, nearly dynamiting him out of his skin. John got vexed, jumped up and gave the brayglock a good kick in the backside, shutting him up in a blink.

The two tourists fell strangely silent, as if in mourning over this remembered sin, and Butu followed suit and stopped muttering and fidgeting as they waited for the solemn mood to pass.

Finally, Elder McIntyre could stand the suspense no longer. "So", he prompted, "Joe expel dem from Paradise just like Adam and Eve."

"Oh, no," the tourist woman laughed, "he forgave them. In fact, they live two doors down from us."

"They're very good neighbours," added the tourist man. "In fact, they keep a brayglock as a pet. It brays for Joe all the time."

"Forgave!" Mad Woman Bellamy sputtered. "Why? Dey disobeyed! Joe said, 'Any of my creatures canst thou kick, except the brayglock, whose sound is beloved to me. Him thou must not kicketh.' Why didn't he burn de disobedient brutes in hellfire?"

"Because he loves them," said the man.

"No fire? No hardship? No expelling?" Elder McIntyre said, looking astonished.

"He loves them," the man repeated.

It is impossible to describe in a preliminary report such as this the effect of this revelation on the assembled Butu. But I could feel their anger building. Even the truck driver, who remained handcuffed on the ground, grew irate.

He said, "Den how come dem get forgive and we get expel from Paradise to rough and tough Jamaica? What kind o' uneven treatment is dat?"

"Is because we black," muttered the atheistic boy, trying to start trouble.

Just then, and to this day I do not know whether the timing was deliberately chosen to vex up Butu some more or whether it was a coincidence, the tourist man cocked his head as if listening to something and said to his companion, "It's Joe. He's having a little birthday party for you this evening."

"Oh, good!" chirped the tourist woman. "I'll wear my new dress."

"Just a minute," I said. "This investigation is not yet concluded. I still need to take statements from both of you."

"Sorry," the tourist man said. "We do have to run. Here, have a look. Guests are already arriving."

He was pointing to a shiny patch of grass under a guinep tree, and as I looked it became like a window on another world, and I beheld (sorry to sound Biblical but I did behold what I beheld) a stream of festively clad revellers strolling across acres of lawns and gardens and entering the open front door of an enormous mansion. Butu surrounded me in a crush, gaping and gasping with amazement and passing comment.

"Look 'pon de big house!"

"What a way dem people dress up like puss back foot!"

"Dem look sharp, eh!"

The man glanced at his wristwatch, said something to the woman, and they both turned to face the crowd.

"We really have to go," said the man.

"Goodbye!" the woman said with a friendly wave.

Then the two of them – and I can imagine how this statement will look in the final official report – stepped atop the window through which we had gotten a glimpse of the assembling birthday celebrants and slipped smoothly into the earth, like they were sliding down a chute.

Two Butu who were nearby screamed, "Me want go, too!" and leapt on the very spot where the man and woman had disappeared, but instead of vanishing, they tumbled on the ground, flat on their faces.

The stunned silence that followed was broken by one of the fallen Butu. He got to his feet, dusted himself off, and said glumly, "How come we God so rough wid we when Joe so nice to dem?"

"Is because we black," said another malcontent.

Another fitful silence fell over them, broken by an unknown voice deep in their midst that said, "I feel like I want burn down something."

An unidentified voice cried, "Make we burn down a church!"

"Which church?" another voice asked.

"Any church," a third said. "Dey all belong to God."

"Dere's one right down de street," yet another Butu yelled.

From the crowd came a deep, bellowing roar, like a lion gone mad, and a spirit of frenzy swept over them.

"Make us burn its rass!" someone shrieked, and the mob took to its heels and stampeded for the church which was in a hollow about a quarter mile away.

It was in vain that I shouted at the rampaging Butu that arson was a criminal offence, for they had all run off and I was left utterly alone at the scene of the accident with only Nurse Spaulding and the truck driver I had earlier subdued.

The driver began bawling for his release. I saw that, in view of the victim's recovery, no crime had been committed and, seeing smoke billowing from the hollow where the church is located, I made the decision to release him so I could be free to investigate the arson in progress.

The driver, once free, tore down the street towards the burning church, bawling, "Me want burn church, too!" and disappeared.

I decided to assess the situation as our training manual recommends and was laying out mentally a course of action for apprehending and arresting the arsonists, when from the direction of the church came a loud shouting for help, to which I and Nurse Spaulding immediately responded.

We found the church completely consumed in flames and the arsonists gathered in a clump around Mad Woman Bellamy, who lay stricken on the ground.

"She's having a heart attack," Nurse Spaulding said, kneeling beside the old woman.

"Is God punishing we for burning his property!" a sister cried.

This pronouncement had an immediate effect on the rioters. Many fell to their knees, crying for forgiveness.

Mad Woman Bellamy, obviously in severe pain, said, "God, is Elder McIntyre put me up to it."

"Mad Woman Bellamy," Elder McIntyre bawled from where he knelt nearby, "no tell God no lie 'pon me! Is you first say, 'Make me go burn a church'."

Mad Woman Bellamy protested in a feeble voice, "Jesus Christ! What a way you lie! Poor, poor me never say nothing 'bout ..."

She obviously had more to say and no doubt would have said it, too, except that she gave a horrible groan, scratched vainly at her chest and died on the spot. Nurse Spaulding applied CPR to no avail. She was dead.

"Repent!" screamed Elder McIntyre at the few sheep left standing. "On you knees! God has sent her soul to hell. She take de Lord's name in vain and didn't repent before she dead. Repent before it's too late for you, too, oh sinful sheep!"

At this exhortation, the remaining hold-out Butu fell on their knees and began a hysterical praying, like baaing sheep.

It is not true that I said to Elder McIntyre, "Hush up you mouth or I going shoot your rass." But I'm sorry I didn't.

The manual says that filers of a preliminary report should strive to use an objective and dispassionate tone, but that personal assessment or opinion of the investigating constable may be noted if its relevancy to the investigation is clearly established.

Personally, it is my opinion that Mad Woman Bellamy's passing was not occasioned by divine revenge but by the excitement and frenzy attendant on the act of arson she helped her fellow Butu brethren commit against the church which was, by the way, a total loss. The woman was eighty-seven years old, and arson is a young man's crime. This opinion, moreover, is seconded by the attached autopsy report, which states that the cause of death was arteriosclerosis.

Some critical questions are still unanswered. First, who were the tourists? Second, where did they really come from? Third, how did they enter the island without proper papers? Fourth, what was their real purpose in visiting Jamaica? Fifth, where did they stay while in Jamaica? Sixth, what immigration laws were broken? Until such factual questions are answered, no charges can be filed against anyone.

It is no use, in this investigator's opinion, asking other questions such as: Who is Joe? What is his true relationship with these people? Such questions are more properly the subject of a theological inquiry, being religious questions on which the government cannot be expected to take an official position.

In keeping with the new reporting protocol, which asks that filers of a preliminary report also compose a suggested final report that will, if approved, become part of the public record, I am including with this, on a separate sheet, a recommended final report.

Recommended Final Report.
Friday, 15th March, 2002.
District of Ewarton.

A truck travelling at a high rate of speed on the main road linking Ewarton with Bog Walk was reported to have grazed a tourist walking with a companion along the roadside. The driver was not charged but was issued an official warning. Neither tourist was hurt. Neither has been identified.

In an unrelated incident, a deranged elderly female resident of the Ewarton district set fire to a local Pentecostal church.

During the commission of this unlawful burning, the suspect suffered a fatal heart attack. Residents of the district identified the arsonist as one Victoria Bellamy, eighty-seven years old, commonly known as Mad Woman Bellamy. Having no known relatives, the deceased, who lived alone, was transported to a government cemetery for the indigent, where the body was buried. No motive for her crime has been established. A government witness and two gravediggers were present. There were no mourners.

Junior Constable Winston Kelvin Humphreys,
badge # 956, assigned to the district of Ewarton

Preliminary Report to remain confidential.

Official Report approved for posting by Inspector Jordan Hall, Senior Officer in Charge, District of Ewarton Constabulary Command, Parish of St Ann, Jamaica

The Story of the Fifth Boy

THE four boys, armed with home-made slingshots, were on their way to the bush for a bird shoot. Usually there were five, but on this particular day the fifth boy was in bed with bronchitis, a sickness that had plagued him intermittently since infancy.

It was August 1955, so sweltering a day that even the outdoors was as windless and stuffy as the dark belly of a cathedral. Yet in spite of the heat the boys, three of them variant shades of black and one so startlingly white his skin looked painted on, walked with the jauntiness of hunters.

They began the day's shoot always with the same ritual: they scaled the wall of the old fort that overlooked the Montego Bay harbour and fired stones with their slingshots at a petchary nesting in the crowns of the royal palms.

The petchary is a songbird of unfathomable denseness. This one would see the boys coming and, instead of flying away, would deliberately perch on the shaky electric wire that ran between the two royal palms, where it would hop to dodge the fusillade of stones. It was taunting them, or so the boys believed, which only made them more infuriated.

The grey fort, a fossil from the seventeenth century, consisted of a concrete wall which wound like a petrified coil around a hillock, creating a fortified gun emplacement for a menacing battery of fifteen cannons. Now only three guns remained, their muzzles sealed shut with wads of concrete, their cast-iron barrels, clammy with the dewfall of the centuries, still pointing in a ceremonial pose at the entrance to the bay.

In the hillside shadows to the rear of the fort squatted a stone building, its swollen reinforced walls slitted with loopholes. Legends claimed that the building was cursed, that anyone who fired a stone through one of the loopholes would have his arm fly behind his back and stick there forever. Defying this curse had become, for the boys, a test of manhood, and after they wearied of trying to kill the petchary, they would take turns shooting stones at the loopholes to see who could come the closest without being struck down.

Then, looking as raffish and ragtag as homeless urchins, they would troop off into the hills for the day's shoot. They would spend the day aiming their slingshots at the population of small birds, mainly grass tits and yellow breasts, and the occasional ground dove. Around midday they would settle down in the cool puddles of shadows to escape the blazing heat, and they would chat about school and tell lies about girls.

Boys do not talk in a straight line. They buzz erratically, like bees, from one topic to another in a herky-jerky splatter of words. On this particular day, they argued about cricket and horse-racing, about which fifth-former should be on the first-eleven football team, about which tutor at school was the toughest.

One of the boys, Joseph, began bragging about having sex on the beach with Cecilia, a dark-brown girl with East Indian features and glossy black hair so shiny it seemed woven with sunlight.

Two of the boys hooted and laughed as Joseph regaled them with exaggerated claims of his prowess as a lover and told vivid stories about how Cecilia had responded, and what she had cried out when she was under him.

Only the white boy, whose name was Bruce, did not laugh or take part in the raillery. He was a Canadian boy, an only child, whose father had been transferred to Montego Bay two years earlier. A quiet boy, Bruce acted most of the time as if he had blundered into the wrong life and couldn't find his way out.

He did not take part in the banter because he secretly adored Cecilia and kept his dreams about her stored in that private, sunless place where boys hoard their heart's treasures. She belonged to the same Catholic church where he was an altar boy, and every now and again when she took Communion his hand holding the golden paten under her throat would shake. To hear Joseph talk so coarsely about her made him cringe. But he said nothing in her defence. To do so would draw a barrage of teasing and jibes.

Jamaican boys fear gentleness. When gentleness appears among them, they crush it as they would a cockroach.

The boys remained in the shade, talking of this and that. Soon the sun fell towards the sea, and as the shadows of the trees and shrubs stretched out their limbs like supplicating beggars, they stood up and drifted towards the footpath that snaked down the mountain.

On a stretch of flatland sandwiched between two mountain slopes they heard the subterranean rumble of a diesel engine and the crackling of wood. A yellow bulldozer, its erect exhaust pipe puffing out spurts of black smoke that flickered and twitched like the tail of a kite, was chewing a broad swatch through the woodlands, gouging out a trail of uprooted bushes and splintered trees.

In the caged cab sat a sweaty black man, his hands gripping two levers that spurred the machine to roar with rage and lunge at the helpless land and devour it with monstrous bites.

"It's de new road dey're always talking about," Joseph shouted over the thunder of the foraging bulldozer.

The four boys gaped wordlessly as the machine devoured their childhood haunt. Then they drifted away slowly like mourners from a gravesite.

By the time they reached the old fort, the sun was barely peeping over the line of the horizon, and all across the bay the ocean was silting up with darkness. The petchary was still on the wire, warbling a song, as sharp and tinkling as a Communion bell.

More from habit than intent, Bruce took a stone out of his pocket, furled the leather tongue of the slingshot over it, lined up the bird in the centre of the crook, pulled back and fired.

The petchary was in the middle of uncoiling a lacy trill when the stone ripped into its throbbing throat.

A wounded bird falls like a spinning leaf or tumbles through the sky like a pinwheel; a killed one plunges to the ground like a ship's anchor to the ocean bottom, exactly how the petchary fell at the boys' feet that August evening.

They were stunned into temporary speechlessness, their eyes wide with wonder and disbelief, and since as boys they still lived in a misty world that had not yet solidified into the idolatrous certainties of adulthood, it took the spoken word of Joseph to certify the reality of the moment.

"Rass, Bruce!" he cried. "You shoot de petchary!"

"It was an accident," Bruce mumbled, brimming with an immeasurable sadness as he bent down to pick up the dead bird, which was still warm and limp between his fingers.

The other boys crowded around him and gently touched the dead petchary as if they feared awakening it from its sleep.

Night was changing the texture of the bay and coating the air with a lacquer of darkness as the boys separated.

The three dark boys took the road into town where they lived in ramshackle wooden buildings and slept in shared beds. The white one headed towards his house overlooking the sea on the main road, where he had his own room and shared his bed with a teddy bear.

On the way home, Bruce stuffed the petchary gently into a pocket he had emptied of stones, and, after eating a strained dinner in the company of his parents, the dead bird still in his pocket, he went into the backyard where his mother kept a rose bed and used a trowel to dig a deep hole in which he tenderly buried the bird. Carefully smoothing over the dirt to hide the grave, he stood with head bowed and recited the Paternoster, which he'd memorized as an altar boy.

The boys continued to go on their shoots, but without the ritual of the taunting petchary the days did not seem the same, and when the summer was over and the school term started, the world told them that they were too old to be killing small birds with slingshots.

On one of the last hunts, this time with me, the fifth boy, among them, we were trudging up the footpath towards the woodlands whose stony breastbone had been torn open by bulldozers and graders to receive a roadbed when one boy muttered, "I miss de petchary."

"I never meant to kill it," Bruce cried.

"Hush up 'bout it!" Joseph said sternly. "Killing bird is what we bird shooters do."

We plodded on up the hill without speaking, feeling a little foolish, as if we were rehearsing a play that was already over.

Time passed.

The new road took possession of the land like a returned absentee landlord, bringing with it a downpour of private homes, small hotels, office buildings, hairdresser shops and parking lots. Woodlands that had once been the haunts of wild birds and boys were now under the proprietorship of maids, garden boys and guard dogs.

Some months later, Cecilia abruptly transferred to a school in Kingston and went to live with her father. By then a grimy story about her and Joseph, dripping like a piece of meat chewed on by many mouths, was circulating.

After she moved, Bruce descended into a dungeon of isolation and darkness. Always a lonely boy, he kept more and more to himself. I would glimpse him from afar ghosting around the school grounds and we would occasionally wave to one another before he disappeared around a corner. Although we were in the same class, we sat on opposite sides of the room and hardly ever spoke during those days.

One evening he surprised me by stopping at my house after school – we lived within walking distance of each other – and during the next hour, because he was in a rare, talkative mood, we spoke of many things. He told me about that memorable day in August when he had killed the petchary. He told me how and where he had buried it.

Then as abruptly as he had come, he suddenly said, "Well, goodbye," and was gone.

The next morning his father found him hanging from the limb of an ackee tree in the backyard.

A memorial service was held at school, and virtually every boy attended to sing hymns and pray for the soul of Bruce. His body, accompanied by his father and mother, was shipped back to Canada for burial.

During the sad service, I think all of us bird-shooting boys felt like crying – I know I did – but we held ourselves back. I don't know why, but that's just the way Jamaican boys are. They just don't cry.

The days scampered past like sugarcane rats.

One evening, some weeks after the funeral, Bruce's mother phoned my house and asked me to stop by and see her. I went and she showed me a note Bruce had left pinned to his pillow. It read:

> Dear Mummy,
>
> I don't like this place any more. I'm sorry if what I'm about to do hurts you, but there must be something better somewhere for me.
>
> Your son,
> Bruce
> PS Tell my friends that I never meant to kill the petchary.

"What does he mean about the petchary?" she asked, her eyes swollen and red from countless hours of weeping.

I shared with her what Bruce had told me.

"Show me where he said he buried the bird," she said, scorching me with a wild stare.

Together we went into the backyard, and while she shone a shaky flashlight beam, I dug in the rose bed and found the buried petchary. Nature had begun her grisly work, and the petchary had been transformed into a ghastly clump of dirty feathers with two empty eye sockets whose jelly had been devoured by swarms of ants tunnelling into its brain.

When the flashlight beam fell upon the decomposed bird, Bruce's mother gave a loud wail of grief that slashed the night air like a rooster's claw.

She snatched the petchary from me, hurled it into the darkness and bent over in a torrent of sobbing.

As I trudged down the driveway, I spotted on the veranda an immovable form sculpted out of a block of darkness. It was Bruce's father.

I made my way home slowly, thinking about Bruce, his mother's sobbing still raw in my memory.

Bruce told me one day at school that the world had too many words in it, that thousands of them could be thrown away without any loss.

I don't know if that's true.

I only know that we are being swept downstream by a relentless river of time. Ahead is a vast ocean of approaching darkness.

Behind is the flicker of hazy recollection. We huddle marooned in the present, where life is uncertain and filled with constant death.

No longer boys, the four of us have long drifted away from Bruce, the petchary, and that day in August 1955.

All that tethers their memory to this moment is this frail string of words.

Unconventionality

RACHEL Higgins, a simple, devout Jamaican Catholic who had lived all her life respectably in the parish of Manchester, could not fall asleep at nights unless her fingers were cupping her husband's testicles.

No one except her husband of thirty-five years, Thomas, knew about this peculiar fixation – not her six children, who had been reared on the family farm and were now long gone abroad, not even her one sister, who had been her bosom friend and neighbour before passing on two years previously.

How and when she had picked up this peculiar habit she could not even remember, but it had been with her throughout her entire marriage.

During the daylight hours, Rachel had the healthy disdain of the old-time wife for her husband's private parts and would no more think of touching his testicles than of petting a cockroach. On those rare occasions when she and Thomas happened to take a nap together in the afternoon, she was able to doze quite well empty-handed. It was only when night fell that she needed a handful of testicles to help her sleep.

The Higginses had lived placidly this way for years. Then, during one terrible stretch of three months, Thomas's friends began dropping dead in droves.

In that terrible three-month period of merciless carnage, the Higginses attended five funerals, mainly for old school chums. Then their next-door neighbour died suddenly of a stroke, depriving Thomas of his closest bird-shooting companion, a man of exactly his own age, and who resembled him so much that strangers often mistook them for brothers.

Thomas began to worry about his own mortality and the fate of his immortal soul.

He started going to Mass regularly, an observance which, like many Catholic men, he'd fallen out of in his middle years. He offered his services to the choir, even though he was tone deaf. He attended a novena – for the first time in ages – and began quietly to say his prayers at night, which was most unlike him.

One night, after whispering prayers as they lay abed, Thomas suddenly became conscious of Rachael cuddling up beside him and reaching for her helping of bedtime testicles, and the juxtaposition between the quiet piety he had just observed and her groping startled him so much that he shied away from her touch.

"What happen?" Rachel wondered, surprised.

"I just finish saying me bedtime prayers," Thomas mumbled crossly.

"Oh," she said, still not understanding why he had pulled away but too tired to quarrel. "It's nice to end de day with a prayer."

Then, without further resistance from him, she fumbled for the testicles, located them, encased them gently under her fingers, and promptly fell asleep.

Afterwards Thomas lay awake worrying if there was life after death. He felt rather strongly that he'd worked much too hard to end up as dust. He was thinking particularly about his school days, when Jamaica had still been a colony of England and he, along with every other Jamaican schoolboy of the time, had been viciously forced to memorize hundreds of lines of gory, militaristic British doggerel.

What had been the point of that if every particle of him was to wind up in the belly of a worm?

For a long time he could not fall asleep.

That same month the parish got a new priest – a stern, young, half-Chinese Jamaican whose name was Father Chen and who, although still in his twenties, was of the old school and uncompromisingly severe in his interpretation of Catholic doctrine. He detested the English liturgy and would have much preferred to have been allowed to say the Mass in Latin. He found it abhorrent that Catholics were nowadays encouraged by the Church to chew the consecrated host as if the living God were so much bubblegum. Everywhere around him he beheld and decried the falling away from old-fashioned Catholic doctrine.

In the first sermon Father Chen preached in the small stone chapel set against a grassy hillside in Manchester, he bluntly declared the doctrine that unconventionality was the root of all sin. If one lived a conventional life, one did not sin, for sin was always a departure from convention.

To most of the country parishioners listening that day in the church, the sermon made little sense, but to Thomas it was a revelation, and he began to wonder if over the years he and Rachael had slipped into sinful unconventionality. He had in mind, particularly, the habit of testicle clutching she had fallen into, which definitely struck him as unconventional. Thomas decided to go to confession and put the case to the priest.

He had not been to confession in twenty years, the practice having fallen out of fashion among Catholics. In fact the Church now wishy-washily called confession the Sacrament of Reconciliation, and many of the dioceses did not even offer it regularly.

Father Chen, however, felt strongly that confession should be reinstated and had announced in one of his sermons that he had found an old-time confessional booth abandoned in a back room of the rectory and was having it varnished and was going to return it to service.

There would be no more sitting together of confessor and priest in straight-backed chairs, like guests at a tea party, as was the fashion nowadays. Instead, as the custom had been in olden days, the priest would be in a proper confessional booth separated from the confessor by a dark wire mesh signifying the secrecy and shame of sin.

On the first day designated for the new confession, Thomas arrived early, slipped gingerly into the confessional booth, which was more cramped than he remembered it from his boyhood days, and came quickly to the point.

"Bless me, Father," Thomas mumbled, feeling quite self-conscious. "I can't think of any sin I committed lately, but I think I'm committing unconventionality."

There was a long pause on the other side of the dark mesh and the sound of an uneasy scuffling.

"What unconventionality?"

Thomas squirmed. "It's my wife," he said sheepishly. "Every night she holds on to my testicles. And I'm worried dat dat's unconventionality."

"It's definitely dat. It's also concupiscence."

Thomas felt his heart sinking. "Concupise-who?"

"Concupiscence. Abnormal sexual lust."

Thomas chuckled. "Oh, no, it's not dat. We're in our sixties now and hardly do it any more. If we do it once a month, we do it plenty. Is not concupi..., whatever you call it."

"So why does she hold your balls, den?" Thomas could almost feel the scowl of the priest burning through the mesh.

"She says it helps her sleep," Thomas breathed, feeling horribly ridiculous.

"Dat's nonsense! Your testicles are dere for the greater glory of God, not to be used by woman to help her sleep, like tablets."

The priest's tone was so severe that Thomas was momentarily shocked into silence. Finally, after an awkward pause, he managed to say, "We never knew it was wrong until I heard your sermon on unconventionality de other day."

"Well, now you know. And it has to stop."

And to demonstrate the depth of his displeasure, the priest sentenced Thomas to the harsh penance of saying a rosary a day for the next week.

"We can't do dis any more," Thomas announced to Rachel abruptly that night when she reached over for her usual bedtime handful.

"What? What you talking about?" she practically squealed.

"I went to confession, and Father said it's concupi... something. It's very bad."

"But how am I to sleep?"

"You just have to learn a new way of sleeping."

Rachel lay still beside him for a long while. She rolled over on one side, perched there for a few uncomfortable minutes, and then tried the other side. She tried lying on her back, then on her belly, but it was no use. Finally, she made a small harrumphing sound and reached belligerently for his testicles.

Thomas pulled away. "Rachel," he scolded, "behave youself!"

After stewing restlessly at his side, Rachel got up and went into another room to read.

Thomas slept badly, and when he woke up the next morning, he found his wife in the drawing room with yesterday's newspaper scattered around her favourite easy chair, where she said she'd spent an unhappy night in sleepless discomfort.

For the remainder of the day she dragged around the house sluggishly and could get nothing done, she was so exhausted. Thomas was in no better shape, and that afternoon he cut his hand badly as he was sharpening a knife to butcher a goat.

The next night was even worse. Neither one of them could fall asleep. Rachel finally got up and padded into the drawing room to read the newspaper, hoping that Thomas would fall asleep on his own and that she would be able to gently dig out his testicles and catch a few winks herself. But when she finally sneaked quietly back to bed, she found that Thomas was wearing briefs and sleeping on his belly, and that it was impossible to excavate his testicles without awakening him.

The next morning Thomas found his wife sprawled out uncomfortably on the easy chair in the drawing room, with the newspaper again strewn in disarray all over the floor.

"I wasn't doing anything wrong," she scowled defiantly. "And today me and dis priest going have it out."

Rachel and the priest had it out that afternoon.

She squeezed herself sulkily into the confessional booth and as soon as she had mumbled the introductory prayer, "Bless me, Father, for I have sinned," she abruptly asked, "What business is it of God's how I fall asleep at night?"

Father Chen sniffed and seemed not at all surprised at her outburst. Indeed, his cold tone and manner said he had been expecting her.

"Did you create leviathan?"

"What?"

"Can you make a whale?"

"No, of course not. I'm only a mortal woman. I can't even make a fly. All I do ..."

"I know what you do. And God doesn't like it. God made all testicles, and God thinks it's concupiscence to be holding dem at night. And God wants it stopped."

Feeling dreadfully sinful and dirty, Rachel was so upset and worn out from sleeplessness that she became tongue-tied and began to cry.

Father Chen's tone softened. He said many consoling things. He told her that God had created testicles so that couples could have children, not for women to play with, and that idly using her husband's testicles as her playthings would bring drought and bankrupt the already hard-strapped parish farmers.

He said all this in a soothing voice as if he were talking to a child instead of a woman old enough to be his grandmother.

But the more he talked, the more inconsolable Rachel became and the louder she wailed until her sobs drifted out into the chapel, making the waiting penitents wish that they could overhear what monstrous sin was being aired out in the confessional booth right under their noses.

She was dispirited and defeated when she got home. Thomas sat in the drawing room with her while an evening mist began curdling over the surrounding rolling fields.

Rachel looked small and old. Thomas noticed for the first time that her hands were shaking.

"I didn't sleep a wink last night," she moaned listlessly as she sat scrunched down in her usual chair. "I read de whole newspaper. I read de want ads. I know who's looking for job as a domestic. I read de ship movements. I know which ship is sailing for Panama and which is headed for Miami. I read de legal notices. I know who getting divorced and who not paying whose bills. I heard a patou all night. Him started hooting at two o'clock and him stop at quarter after three. Meanwhile, I didn't sleep a wink. If dis keep up, I soon dead."

Thomas sighed, felt pity for his aging wife, and gave up.

"Come to bed, dearest," he said, extending his hand to her. "Come help me sleep."

"I can't," she cried, wracked by sobs. "I'll put your soul in jeopardy. I'll cause drought. I'll bring bankruptcy to de district. I'll ruin de poor farmers."

"If I don't get some sleep, I'll have a heart attack and die."

"So, in a way, I'd be saving your life. I'd be doing a good deed for me husband," she sniffed in a hopeful voice, looking pleadingly up at him.

"Exactly! For dis kind of penance, a woman's soul could go straight to heaven."

They hurried off to bed, even though it was barely past eight o'clock, and as they settled down, Rachel gathered up a handful of testicles with a sigh and seemed as if she would drop off immediately. But Thomas became unexpectedly aroused, and they ended up making love – the first time in months.

Afterwards, with the testicles damp and spongy under her fingers, like freshly laid pigeon's eggs, Rachel cuddled up next to her old husband and wondered aloud if they would go to hell for the concupi-whatever-it-was sin they had committed tonight.

Outside, an enormous ancient night had blotted out the visible countryside, and all that was left of the day was shattered bone dust of starlight sprinkled throughout the bottomless sky.

They fell asleep, with hell very much on their minds, but for the first time in two nights, they slept soundly and awoke to a morning like one of those from childhood days when the young earth was always fresh with innocence and loveliness.

Still troubled about the unconventionality of what they had done, Thomas was determined to take up the doctrine again with the priest and plead for a reinterpretation.

However, before he could, news reached the Higginses that Father Chen had been killed in a car crash on Spur Tree Hill. He had been returning to the rectory late at night after spending the whole day in Santa Cruz hearing old-fashioned confessions at the request of the local deacon and had fallen asleep at the wheel.

The Higginses attended a memorial Mass for the repose of the dead priest's soul. One old lady parishioner, who had been particularly fond of the half-Chinese priest, burst into a loud wailing during the funeral and screeched that the priest had been a saint who would return triumphantly with the angelic hordes on Judgment Day.

A few weeks later, a new priest was assigned to the diocese. He was a stout, middle-aged Irishman from the liberal wing of the Church, who loved rum, laughing and his belly. The first thing he did was to retire the confessional booth to the cobwebs in the back room where it had formerly been stored.

When Thomas gingerly put the case to him about a hypothetical cousin (from another parish) whose wife could not sleep unless she was holding her husband's testicles, the new priest burst into a belly-laugh and declared the Church to be fully supportive of wifely testicle holding, so long as the testicles were unhanded by said lawful wife an hour before she took Communion, to show respect for the Eucharist.

When Thomas wondered whether the same unnamed cousin (from another parish) could unwittingly be bringing drought (to her parish) with her unconventional testicle holding, the priest guffawed and said that drought was caused by a stationary upper-level high pressure system, not by anything so local and idiotic.

Although badly confused by the priest's explanation of drought, Thomas was, nevertheless, elated.

He hurried home to share the splendid doctrinal news with Rachel who, when she heard, danced around her favourite drawing room easy chair for sheer schoolgirlish joy.

A Sign of the Times

AFTER a long, hard day of battering about the streets of Kingston, the Rawlstons invariably ended up each evening sitting on their veranda, taking stock of these wicked times.

The Rawlstons were in their later middle years, brown, and quite convinced that their way of life was superior to the hurly-burly behaviour they saw emerging among the up-and-coming generation of younger Jamaicans.

One evening they settled down as usual on their veranda and began the daily stocktaking.

Mrs Rawlston opened by citing an example of the forwardness of this worthless generation, bred like so many flies during the socialist rot of the 1970s. She was the head bookkeeper of an insurance firm, and she had instructed a newly hired clerk to post a certain item of expense in a particular account.

"Why must dat go dere, Mrs Rawlston?" the girl had dared to ask.

Here Mrs Rawlston threw her back upright in a spasm of indignation, cocked her head, aimed her mouth point-blank at her attentive husband and blasted him with the reply she'd used that morning to broadside the ignorant twit.

"Why must dat go dere?" she mimicked in a petulant tone. "It must go dere because I say it must go dere. Must every little order bring about an examination of company policy? Is my word not sufficient?"

"Indeed," chorused her husband dutifully, bobbing his head like a churchgoer during repentant testimony, "Jamaicans ask too much question nowadays. What happened to doing as you're told?"

"Dere's just too much 'why' in Jamaica today," Mrs Rawlston said gravely. "Everything is why, why, why."

Mrs Rawlston carried on a bit more about the episode, adding some imaginary remarks she wished she had thought of at the time to the fusillade she'd actually delivered, and when she was done, she was so breathless that she had to stop and gasp the stale Kingston breeze that was wafting over the veranda. All around them the sporadic chatter and shrieks of the demented age provided a background rattle that splattered over them like gravel.

Mrs Rawlston having run out of breath, Mr Rawlston took his turn at bat. "Why is this generation of Jamaicans so hopelessly lazy?" he asked, thus proposing his own theme for the evening. He was a contractor currently building a house for an expatriate Jamaican, and he began morosely to tell a tale about what had happened that day at the construction site.

A truck had delivered a load of building blocks, and his labourers were required to unload the blocks and cart them in wheelbarrows down to the structure.

One man had repeatedly bawled, "Lawd, sah, de load heavy!"

"Heavy!" Mr Rawlston had scoffed. "You don't see heavy yet!"

Another worker quit in the middle of the job, saying that loading up the blocks had made him tired of Jamaican life, and he intended to go immediately to the American Embassy and apply for an immigration visa. A third claimed he had hurt his back and left the site saying he was going to file a Worker's Compensation Claim at the doctor's office.

To cope with all this rampant malingering and to set a good example, Mr Rawlston said modestly, he himself had stepped up to the truck and unloaded blocks onto the wheelbarrow.

"See!" he had taunted the complaining worker, when he could find the breath, "Dis is how man load a wheelbarrow, you lazy brute you."

"What is Jamaica coming to," Mrs Rawlston moaned, "dat de boss has to show de worker how to do de work?"

"Is a sign of de times," Mr Rawlston replied glumly.

They fulminated for another hour or so but then were soon done, for their bedtime was stalking them, and they had a habit of retiring promptly every night at the same hour.

Before he went to bed, Mr Rawlston made the rounds, latching windows and locking doors, for the Kingston night breeze sometimes blew menace and wickedness over innocent, law-abiding householders. Sealed up inside their small house, the veranda caged in and bolted shut with a wrought-iron birdhouse frame, the Rawlstons went to bed.

Sometime around two, Mr Rawlston stirred. He thought he had heard a noise. He lay still and rigid in the bed and only his right eyelid stealthily inched open. He took a cautious peek around the dark room and saw two monstrous, burly shadows lurking nightmarishly at his bed-foot.

Mr Rawlston did not move a muscle even though his heart was exploding in his ears and drumming loud enough, he felt, to awaken the dead. And he would have remained that way for the rest of the night, until the darkness had swallowed up the intruders, had not Mrs Rawlston awoken, too, and emitted a tiny squeak of terror while pretending to be cemented by sleep to her pillow. But the men had heard. They knew.

The overhead light snapped harshly on.

"Get up!" one thief ordered with a hiss.

The other cocked a gun with a metallic click of doomsday and death. The Rawlstons jerked upright in bed, eyes gaping, quivering in a spasm of pyjamas and clinging bed sheets.

"Scream and you dead!" the first thief growled, pointing a bigger gun steadily at Mrs Rawlston's broad, rounded forehead.

"Everything we have is yours, sah!" Mrs Rawlston begged. "Take anything you want, only spare life!"

"Yes, sah! Do!" Mr Rawlston agreed, nodding vigorously.

"Look in me purse under de chair cushion," Mrs Rawlston invited. "Money is dere. Every dollar is yours. Take it, sah!"

The thief who was obviously in charge shuffled over to the chair, emptied the purse and counted out the bills.

"Dis is all you have?" he grumbled.

"No, sah!" Mrs Rawlston said breathlessly, as though she had just remembered something wonderful. "I have a little something under de bed I was saving for me retirement."

She flattened herself out onto the floor, crawled halfway under the bed and shakily emerged with a sheaf of bills, many of them soiled and badly crumpled and looking as if they had never seen daylight. The head thief counted out the money in the splotchy yellow overhead light, but was still not satisfied, muttering that she must have been planning to have a very short retirement if this was what she was expecting to live on.

"De time hard," Mr Rawlston muttered in his wife's defence, "and money tough to come by."

The thieves looked as if they were unsure about what to do next, and while the Rawlstons trembled beside their bed, the two criminals muttered between themselves, occasionally casting dubious glances at the terrified homeowners.

Eventually, the thief with the bigger gun announced that life would be spared tonight, but that everything in the house would have to be taken to make up for the pitiful shortage of household funds. Otherwise, the night would not have been worth the effort.

"And", the second thief interposed officiously, "you both going have to load up de truck."

"You want *me* to load a truck?" Mrs Rawlston carped impulsively. "Why? I'm a woman."

"Because I say so," snapped the thief surlily. "Don't question my orders."

"Jamaicans ask too much damn question nowadays," the head thief growled. "What happen to de old days when people did as dey were told?"

"Dem days dead and gone, massah," his companion said sympathetically. "Now everything is why, why, why."

And so it was that the Rawlstons were forced, at gunpoint, to unplug all their appliances and carry them, along with portable items of furniture, on their heads or cradled in their arms and load them into the back of a pick-up truck parked in the shadow of their house.

As he was in the midst of lugging the television set across the drawing room, Mr Rawlston moaned, "Lawd Jesus, what a way de load heavy!"

"Lazy brute!" the head thief snapped. "You don't see heavy yet!"

When it became evident that Mr Rawlston was overburdened and in danger of dropping and shattering the television set, the second thief showed him how it should be carried – diagonally, by the corners, where he could secure a good handhold.

"What a hell," the head thief complained. "See what Jamaica come to! You have to show dem how to do every little thing! Jamaicans are de laziest people on earth. Dey don't want to work. All dey want do is migrate."

"Is so people lazy nowadays," the lieutenant thief lamented, shaking his head. "Now," he said brusquely to Mr Rawlston, "pick up the TV and get back to work. And I don't want to hear any bawling about heavy load, either, you lazy brute you."

"Yes, sah," Mr Rawlston whimpered.

For the next two hours, until nearly four o'clock in the morning, the Rawlstons were forced to load up the thieves' pick-up truck with nearly every stick of furniture they possessed, until the poor truck, burdened by their worldly goods, was sagging visibly, and every time Mrs Rawlston tried to put in a word of pleading for one item or another that had a special sentimental value to her, she was gruffly told not to question thief policy but to be content with carrying out her particular task in life without shirking or griping about it, if she knew what was good for her.

It was after four o'clock in the morning when the pick-up sputtered off into the night, leaving the Rawlstons' bedroom stripped naked of everything but their bed and their dresser. The Rawlstons crawled under the bed, counting themselves blessed for having escaped certain death, and hid quivering there, hugging each other up and trying their best to avoid being hysterical.

The next morning Mrs Rawlston went to the doctor, complaining of an aching back from the heavy loads she'd been forced to lift at gunpoint. While there, she inquired of the nurse whether or not she could file a Workman's Compensation Claim for the injury she had received, which, although incurred because of criminal activity, was definitely work-related.

Mr Rawlston, for his part, drove down to the American Embassy to apply for an immigration visa.

Absentee Ownership of Cows

ONE Saturday morning Mr Alfred Hutchins, an elderly Jamaican living abroad in Georgia, received a mystifying letter from a cow. The envelope it came in bore the return address of "Bamboo PO, St Ann," the parish in Jamaica from which Mr Hutchins and his family had migrated to America twenty-four years before and in which he had always dreamed of living out his last days.

He had been slowly building a squat concrete-block cottage on a hillside of St Ann's, and eventually, he told himself repeatedly, he would leave America and settle down in it while he still had good years left. But the day never came. Now his wife was dead and buried behind the cottage, his two children were long gone, and his few remaining friends were self-absorbed in their own infirmities. He himself was retired and wasting away in idleness.

Mr Hutchins was a stout, elderly brown gentleman whose shuffling absent-mindedness made him seem like a commuter who'd mistakenly stepped off at the wrong bus stop. And when the letter from the cow arrived, he had been typically dawdling away the morning in the drawing room of his Decatur, Georgia, house.

He read the letter surrounded by the bric-a-brac of a long domestic life: photographs, keepsakes and stitchery samplers scattered on the walls and tabletops of the room as if stranded there by a receding tide.

After the letter had sunk in, Mr Hutchins bawled out aloud, his brown face crinkled with astonishment, "Me God, Thelma! A cow write me!"

"Cows can't write, Alfred," he heard Thelma Hutchins snip from the right side of his head, where since her funeral she had squatted illegally, like a hooligan on idle government land. "You know dat."

"Maybe so, but dis letter sounds like it really could come from de pen of a cow. Listen!" And he read the letter in the gruff voice he imagined would suit a Jamaican bush cow with a secondary school education:

> Bamboo PO,
> St Ann,
> Jamaica,
> West Indies.
> 20 February, 2000
>
> Dear Mr Hutchins,
> Nineteen years ago you left me tied to a tree and traipsed away to live in America. In all that livelong time of absentee ownership, you have scarcely visited me. Even when you did visit, each time you complained that I was failing to get fat enough to satisfy. I hereby deplore such shabby treatment. Slavery days are well past, and although the world views me as a humble cow, I still have ambition. I am therefore asking you to return to Jamaica for the purpose of releasing me from despicable absentee ownership and correcting unsatisfactory past treatment.
>
> Yours faithfully,
> A. Cow

"'Traipsed away to America!'" Mr Hutchins bellowed indignantly, the empty house amplifying his words like a megaphone. "We never traipsed! We migrated to escape socialism!"

"Alfred," Thelma reminded him, "dis is de word of a good-for-nothing cow."

"Cow, what? Dis is from no cow! When you ever hear cow write a sentence like, 'despicable absentee ownership and correcting unsatisfactory past treatment'? Dat sound like cow writing to you?"

"I wouldn't know. I am not a good judge of cow phrasing."

"I can't stand de way you get sarcastic ever since you dead! And you used to have such a pleasing personality! Now comes death and turns you bitter."

Before Mrs Hutchins could sting him with a tart reply, Mr Hutchins hurried to the window and drew the drawing room curtains.

It had occurred to him that an inquisitive native-born American passer-by might look in, see a retired immigrant gesticulating to himself and mistake him for mad, when all he was doing was waging everyday domestic argument with a wife lodged in his head who gave him no peace.

Mr Hutchins did not trust Americans. He did not understand them. Even after living among them for over two decades, they still mystified him with their scandalous goings-on as reported on the news. Next thing you knew the authorities would think that he was barricading (a term Mr Hutchins never understood) and send a police sniper to shoot him down in his own front doorway.

The argument ran its course until the noonday sun caused the shadows to furl up their hems tightly, and the trees, cars, shrubs and small houses in the neighbourhood sported the skimpy batty-rider outfits of slack dance-hall sisters.

It was hot inside the house, this being July. Outside the becalmed air wavered off the pavement and roadway in crinkled sheets.

Mr Hutchins took out a battered old typewriter his children had used to write term papers for high school courses. He sat down at the dinner table to type a reply.

He began by asking A. Cow to please not take him for a fool. He knew perfectly well that this letter came from no cow but from the hand of a jealous person who envied him his few possessions and his unfinished hillside house. He reminded the beast that he well knew how Jamaicans at home, seething with spite, envied those who had migrated.

He asked the cow who had worked and slaved for umpteen tough years in America; who had suffered hardship, winter, privation, and been driven nearly mad by an ugly nasal twanging in his ears for those said umpteen years; who had endured the scorn heaped on the new immigrant, the evangelical poppy-show of citizenship; who had had to put up with being sneered at by the statue of a battleaxe, armed with a five-ton concrete torch that threatened to bust open the heads of incoming immigrants, crawling ashore looking for honest work.

Certainly not some ambitionless country cow that took the liberty to criticize its rightful owner.

When he had finished the letter he asked Thelma her opinion of it.

She said, "Puss don't business in dog fight," and spitefully withheld her criticisms, remarking that she could not in a clear conscience endorse corresponding with an infra dig cow.

"You know, Thelma," Mr Hutchins said bitterly, "being dead just don't suit you. It just don't suit you!"

And he walked to the nearest postbox where he mailed the letter, chuckling to himself that "A. Cow" probably had expected no reply.

A month passed. It was a dreary, patternless, empty month, fluttering aimlessly past like a dowdy bushland moth. It was a month of old man's days during which nothing happened and almost every hour seemed stark, lonely and companionless.

He went to church with an American widow, watched baseball games and attended a Jamaican association meeting where he could open his heart and chat frankly in patois. Among Jamaicans, Mr Hutchins could draw clean breath and speak his mind freely, knowing that the contraband smuggled deep within the immigrant's heart – that America was a demented land – was shared and understood as well as any axiom of Euclidean geometry. Here Mr Hutchins felt as if he could speak his mind without threat of a clubbing from a concrete Baal, as he called the Statue of Liberty.

During this month, Mr Hutchins circled the American widow, as he had done for the past year.

One night, as she was giving him a perfunctory kiss inside her front doorway, he tried brushing his hand against her rubbery belly when a thunderous box detonated on the side of his head, making his ears ring.

The irate woman pitched him roughly out of the front door and yelled at him that he should be deported for daring to feel up the widow of a war veteran.

As Mr Hutchins scuffled home in the shadows, Thelma awoke, complaining that her neck had been cricked by the thunderclap blow.

"What you do to de woman dat make her nearly kill me in me sleep?"

"I don't understand why she threaten me with deportation," Mr Hutchins grumbled. "Is her belly I feel up, not de government's. If I live to be a hundred, I'll never understand dese American people."

"A war widow's belly is government property!" Thelma snapped. "What you immigrant hand doing 'pon it?"

Mr Hutchins trudged past the darkened rows of small hunched-over houses, wading through brackish pools of illumination puddling on the sidewalk beneath the streetlight posts, towing in his wake an oily shadow that resembled a lumbering, dispirited manatee.

After a month another ill-mannered letter arrived from the cow. It said:

> Pursuant to your recent letter of the 26th ultimo, please be informed that matters remain unsatisfactory and unchanged. Your rope is still fastened around my neck. I am still bound to a heartless tree. The said letter incorrectly states that grass is an owner's only responsibility and makes no mention of patriotism, which is necessary to build a country.
>
> Moral fibre comes from leadership and discipline, not from eating grass. It is the same situation with church-going. Being tied to a tree, I find myself in ever-present danger of backsliding. I repeat: my position cannot be rectified until you repatriate yourself and I am released from the wickedness of colonial and absentee ownership.
>
> I am, sir, yours truly,
> A. Cow

Mr Hutchins was furious. He read and reread the letter over and over again in the small drawing room. "'... grass is an owner's only responsibility and makes no mention of patriotism, which is necessary to build a country.'" Mr Hutchins howled. "Thelma, you hear how dis feisty cow talk to me! Dat's it! I'm going home tomorrow! I'm going to kick dis impertinent cow in him backside!"

"You travelling to Jamaica to kick a letter-writing cow?"

"Leave me alone!" Mr Hutchins wailed. The muslin curtains shuddered with his blast.

"I trying to sum up for you own good ..."

"Don't sum up! I must handle dis my own way! And my way is to kick dis rude-boy cow in him backside!"

He stormed into the bedroom to pack, dogged by Thelma's heartless query, "You going to Jamaica to kick a cow?"

He packed furiously, as if he was beating up the suitcase. He flung trousers and shirts into it, and as he moved feverishly from the bed to the closet and the dresser, he felt the light-heartedness of one who has just made a difficult decision.

When he was done with the packing, he made his flight reservations and sat down to write some letters.

Mr Hutchins had a son and a daughter, both grown and engrossed in their careers in other states, and he spent the long afternoon typing them muddled letters outlining his projected timetable as if they had not already orbited far, far out of reach of his lonely life.

He wrote the American widow a letter explaining that he had not been slyly trying to feel her up, that his hand had brushed her belly by accident, that it was never his intent to fondle government property. He tried a paradox on her, asking rhetorically whether she would have invoked her widowhood if her husband had been shot for cowardice. Would she have bawled at him, "I am de widow of an American coward, and now you come feel up my belly? You should be deported!"

"You're not taking enough clothes," Thelma warned as he tore up the letter and sprinkled the shreds into the trash can.

When the plane landed in Montego Bay, Mr Hutchins's heart pounded with the wayfarer's joy of homecoming, and he was swept by a tide of giddiness and elation.

He stepped slowly down the nubbly metal stairs of the ramp, fondling with his eyes the background ridge of green mountains splotched with hotels and villas, the stretch of swamp in which egrets stepped suspiciously on tiptoe, the endlessly crinkled folds of blue sea. The breezes carried long-remembered childhood scents, and the land itself was as familiar to him as the bosom of a beloved nanny. He trudged across the tarmac, gazing around him in a daze, as a centipedal line of tourists' feet pattered impatiently past him.

He took a taxi to St Ann, chattering with the driver about the old days as the countryside opened up before his eyes like a cherished childhood storybook.

It was dark when they arrived. The night was settling down heavily over the countryside, and with no moon or streetlight in this desolate part of the island, the driver was reluctant to drop the old man off at the unfinished concrete building, shipwrecked against the hillside and surrounded by the rubble of ongoing construction. But Mr Hutchins assured him he was safe, that this was his parish and his land, that here was nothing but the joy and gladness of his childhood haunts.

The van rattled off down the dirt road, its tail lights peering fretfully after Mr Hutchins.

He let himself into the house, pausing in the doorway to listen to whistling frogs piping to the night, croaking lizards clearing their throats like suss-sussing grandmothers, cicadas and crickets singing the songs of cobweb kites in the Christmas breeze.

The house was dark and desolate, and the bare concrete rooms muttered at his footfalls with a friendless echo.

He lit a kerosene lantern, pouring a greasy yellow light into the stark bedroom.

He felt a great weariness, the sort he never used to feel as a young man. He washed his face, undressed and climbed into the small metal bed shuddering beside the plain, unpainted wooden bureau. When he blew out the lantern, an immensity of darkness swamped the room.

It was a "little-little" Jamaican retirement house in which Mr Hutchins had settled down to sleep, erected over the years in fitful stages when money was available. The unfinished second floor was open. Steel rods jutted through the concrete blocks, and the jagged roofless walls of the second floor sucked at the night mists. In the milky wash of starlight the house gleamed against the hillside, looking like an enormous shell.

"Thelma," Mr Hutchins whispered to the darkness, "I come home."

"Me, too, Alfred," she murmured.

"And don't it feel nice to be home, Thelma," Mr Hutchins said in a quavering voice that made him feel foolish and ashamed, "even if it took a cow to bring us back?"

Mr Hutchins wanted to say more, much more, but he was an old-fashioned Jamaican, and his heart could not pour its feelings into his mouth unless he was drunk or drowning in female wailing at a graveside. Under such conditions, a man's heart might crack slightly, making him admit things that in broad daylight would otherwise seem fool-fool. He wanted to ask Thelma whether they had made a terrible mistake migrating to America and growing their children in a strange land among foreign ways and customs when all along they had meant to end their own days at home.

"You know, Thelma," he whispered, "de cow was right. Jamaica give us life. We give our strength, our children to America. And what we give to Jamaica? Our old bones."

Mrs Hutchins said the times had been hard in ways that no country cow would ever understand.

But Mr Hutchins was not satisfied, and as the night mist seeped and coiled through the louvred windows, he murmured, "Mummy, I come home. I sorry I ever leave you. Forgive me."

He thanked God that there was no one alive in the dark room to jeer at his foolishness.

Then he fell asleep.

He was found the next morning by the caretaker in the unfinished bedroom, his dead body lying on its side as if washed up onto the bed sheets during the misty night.

The next week he was laid to rest in a home-made backyard grave beside Thelma. After the internment, a small service of thanksgiving was observed in the village church, for Mr Hutchins had lived so long and prospered so well that it would have been ungrateful to mourn.

His two children briefly attended, gleaming with the crispness of life in a developed country, looking out of place and uncomfortable among the few scruffy village elders who, remembering Mr Hutchins as a school chum, wobbled at the lip of his grave, hands clasped gravely behind their backs.

Among the mourners was the village postmistress, who knew

Mr Hutchins only as a friend of her father's. As boys, the two old men had romped barefoot together, and before his own passing her father had told her many night-time stories about their care-free boyhood escapades and adventures. That is why she did not tell the foreign children about the demented letter their father had posted to an "A. Cow", which she had opened under her duly constituted authority as postmistress when it had been unclaimed.

He had been a lonely old man in his final days, and his brain had begun to sputter. How else to explain the lunacy of writing a letter of rebuke to a cow? How else to account for his angry belief that the cow had provokingly written to him first?

How else?

The Dog

THE migration of the Leylands from Jamaica to America, some forty years previously, had taken them on a journey through geographic space and economic categories. In 1959 they arrived in New York dirt poor. Ten years later they were doing well. Five years after that, they had become comfortable, and another five years on, well off. By the time their two sons had entered college the Leylands were rich.

Counting their house and some vacation properties they owned in different states, as well as their annuities and stock market investments, cars, furniture, personal effects and bank accounts, their net worth amounted to just under twenty million dollars.

There were two Leylands, Horace and Matilda, a black couple in their late fifties, married for thirty-seven years, neither one particularly a lover of money. They did not live lavishly nor spend foolishly and never indulged their appetites. Horace did not hunt. He belonged to no country clubs, did not play golf and had no expensive hobbies. He was neither yachtsman, powerboater nor womanizer. In fact, he made it quite plain that he loved only one woman, and that was Matilda.

As for Matilda, she sat beside her husband in exactly the same uncushioned rowboat. She was not a show-off, did not care whether or not she dressed fashionably and associated expensive jewellery with sin and Jezebel. She drove a five-year-old car (poor Horace, for the sake of image, was saddled with a new Mercedes) which she was quite fond of and had no plans to buy another until this one was quite dead.

So the Leylands got no thrill from what money could buy or where money could take them. They were happy being at home in the company of each other and, except for occasional trips to Jamaica and the village of their birth and childhood, they went nowhere.

Yet money clung to them like mud to a hog. Both liked to play with money the way Jamaican boys like to play marbles or girls like to play jacks. They loved making money grow for its own sake, and both got an equal chance of cultivating it. When Horace made an investment, it was as if some prophetic duppy voice inside him was telling him unerringly what to do. Matilda, on the other hand, made her moves in the money game like a natural athlete, by sheer instinct. The result was that over the years, and without meaning to, they had made more money than they could spend in the years remaining.

But to the Leylands, this accumulation of money was a little embarrassing and mattered in only one way: in score-keeping.

All immigrants have the feeling of being players in some global sport watched by a gallery of old teachers, aunts, uncles and cousins, former boyfriends and girlfriends, to say nothing of acquaintances. In this unacknowledged game, the score-keeping was computed not in runs, as in cricket, but in money. And so far the Leylands had a score of twenty million, not out.

When they went home, they were like triumphant batsmen in a cricket test match who were on a tea break. Naturally, both were modest about their turn at the wicket. But Jamaicans knew a good knock when they saw one, and wherever the Leylands travelled throughout their childhood haunts, they met with respect and admiration.

With their sixtieth decade bearing down on them, the Leylands now found themselves in the usual danger of jumping economic categories, this time from rich to filthy rich.

The leap depended on the acceptance of an offer Horace had made in a complicated corporate stock deal. It entailed a risky investment of fifteen million cash, but with strong prospects for increasing their wealth to several hundred million.

Should this mega-deal succeed, Matilda would not buy a new car. Horace would not buy a yacht, and neither one would take a trip to Kathmandu. But it would establish them as the greatest scoring duo of any Jamaican batsmen ever to make a stand on the fantasy field of immigration cricket.

The imagined applause of the gallery was, to the Leylands, intoxicating.

The Leylands lived in Baldwin Hills, an upscale suburb of Los Angeles occupied exclusively by black professionals and brown well-to-do's. Their house was sturdy and attractive with tidy gardens and geometrically laid out flower beds, but little different from any other in the neighbourhood.

Here one morning, in their spacious, well-lit designer kitchen, the Leylands were taking a light breakfast. Horace was at the kitchen counter, sitting on a stool and eating a muffin. Matilda was nearby, drinking coffee and behaving as though her mind had flown off to the dark side of the moon.

She paced the kitchen restlessly, exchanging small talk with her husband in a vague, circling way that told him she had something more weighty to discuss but couldn't quite get to the point.

Finally, she stopped her circling, landed on a nearby stool at the kitchen counter, and said, "Horace, I've been thinking."

"I can see dat," he said. "What's wrong?"

"I'm worried," she admitted with a fretful sigh, picking at her chin nervously. "Do you remember old lady Stephenson?"

It took Horace only a second or two for a face and story matching that name to come bubbling up from his stock of childhood memories.

Old lady Stephenson had lived on a small farm just outside May Pen, Clarendon, near the village where the Leylands were born and raised. When she was sixty-five, by some stunning luck, she won fifty thousand pounds, then an unimaginable sum of money, in the Irish sweepstakes, catapulting her and her district into a state of delirium. Being a generous old soul, she was in the middle of making plans to host an all-night fete for everyone she knew when she was felled by a stroke and paralysed for life. The next day, the cheque arrived by special courier, who delivered it at the old lady's hospital bed, where she lay in a coma.

For years afterwards that sad case was the talk of the entire parish of Clarendon. Having recalled the story, Horace immediately understood where the discussion was leading. He nibbled his muffin and waited for her explanation.

Matilda sighed and fidgeted with a kitchen towel.

Her Jamaican childhood had taught her many lessons, some of which she had jettisoned in her journey from Jamaica to America and from a young woman of twenty to a matron of fifty-nine. But one central belief she had kept constantly in her heart: life was an untrustworthy, ill-tempered dog. It would bite at the slightest provocation. It had its stalking patterns and a streak of viciousness that could erupt without warning. One of its favourite patterns was to create the illusion that everything was going well, lull the unwatchful Jamaican into complacency, and then leap up and tear open his throat.

No adult had ever sat Matilda down and said as much. But in an accumulation of gestures and bitter remarks made over the years, the lesson had nevertheless been taught.

Her mother, for instance, whenever she heard of awful tragedy used to shake her head as though she had glimpsed a profound inevitability, and lament, "A so life stay", meaning that's how life was. Matilda had never seen her mother openly, exuberantly happy, happy with an abandonment of caution and a fullness of spirit. Jamaican people were, instead, always cautiously, circumspectly happy, so as not to draw the dog's attention.

With different nuances and in slightly different words, Horace had also been given a man's dosage of this same lesson, enough for him to know exactly what Matilda meant and to catch his own whiff of the danger.

A long moment passed while each Leyland contemplated the emerging pattern that appeared to have sprung up around them stealthily, like a growth of poisonous mushrooms.

"So you saying", Horace asked, as if he didn't know exactly what she meant, "dat things going too well?"

Matilda flinched and nearly said, "Shhh." Some things should be whispered, not openly discussed in a voice that might be overheard. She sighed again as though faced with both doom and mystery.

"Look at us ...," she said in almost a whisper. "We're so ..." She could not bring herself to say the word "happy", that would have been like waving a piece of raw meat right under the dog's nose. Instead, she said, "We're so all right. We've been all right for years now. Barry is finishing his Ph.D. in mathematics at Harvard. And Lennie is teaching at MIT, teaching physics to ..." she almost said "white people" but didn't want to be provocative.

But Lennie *was* teaching the mysteries of physics to white people and *was* held in such high esteem by his colleagues and fellow physicists – and the child only twenty-seven – that he was being considered by a Nobel Laureate as a key researcher in a hush-hush project so secret that the government denied its existence. If accepted, Lennie himself would one day be in a position to win a Nobel prize. What was even more frightening was the ease with which the child's life had unfolded – twenty-seven years old, a natural brain and not even a scratch on his handsome young black body.

Then there was Barry, on a full scholarship to Harvard, where he studied mathematics and, although only twenty-four, had already done something remarkable to *pi*. Exactly what he had done to *pi* Matilda didn't know, but whatever it was had earned him a mention in *Time* magazine, where his picture had appeared above the caption of "Afro-American mathematician makes breakthrough".

A mood of reflective sombreness, the way people feel before a funeral, had settled over the kitchen and the Leylands. Horace recalled other cases of Jamaicans who had been riding high one minute and torn to pieces the next. Matilda quietly sifted through her own inventory, like an archaeologist combing through fragments of dinosaur teeth.

" Well," Horace finally said, "we've been all right for years. So have many other people. So what? Dere's no need for panic."

"True," Matilda eagerly agreed. She paused, and in that pause came the ancient fear of the dog. She remembered what the dog had done to her uncle, beloved younger brother of her mother, who had spent a lifetime looking for the ideal wife only to be murdered on his honeymoon.

Matilda shuddered and sucked at the air with an audible gasp as though she was having trouble breathing.

The phone rang. Horace answered it.

"Hello," he said in his investor's voice.

"Really?"

He gestured to Matilda and formed the name "Lennie" silently with his lips. After listening for an eternity, or so it seemed to Matilda, he said, "Wonderful. Don't forget to call and tell your mother."

He put down the handset carefully as though it was an egg.

"Lennie says he's been asked to join de research project as a fully accredited researcher with top secret clearance," Horace said heavily.

In her mind, Matilda saw the dog lift its head and sniff the breeze for prey.

"Why can't he just teach physics like normal people, eh?" she asked querulously.

"He's too bright to do only dat," said Horace.

"I suppose dat's my fault," Matilda said bitterly.

'No, it isn't," Horace corrected gently. "It's mine."

"What are you saying, Horace?" She was staring stonily at him.

"Maybe we should start going to church," Horace muttered lamely.

Both Leylands disliked attending church with such passion that this drastic suggestion made Matilda gasp with shock.

"You think it's dat serious?" she asked in a pleading tone.

The phone rang again. Horace answered it eagerly. This call was even shorter than the first and at least as cryptic, and when Horace hung up the phone, he said heavily, "Barry has made another mathematical breakthrough in *pi*. He didn't have time to get into it because there're television reporters waiting downstairs. He's going to be on CNN tonight."

"What is wrong with dat boy?" Matilda asked, making an impatient gesture as if she was trying to thump down someone invisible. "Why can't he leave dat damn *pi* alone? I'm sick to death of all de bad news."

Horace got off the stool and began pacing in circles around his wife, like an ever-tightening noose. He stopped and snapped his fingers.

"What if dey don't accept our offer?" he asked. "It would definitely be a setback."

Matilda brightened visibly. "Maybe," she said hopefully, reaching for the moon, "we'll even lose de fifteen million!"

"Dat would leave us only five million to live off of," Horace said, his spirits rising.

"Wouldn't dat be lovely? But we'd manage. We wouldn't have to sell de house or anything dat drastic, but I could cut down on groceries by clipping coupons and shopping de sales."

"I could sell de Mercedes and share your car," Horace vowed, falling into the spirit of exultancy. "Of course, it might not be necessary. Five million is still a lot of money."

"Now, don't ruin everything with your goat mouth," she scolded, reminding him of the Jamaican belief that the mouth of the goat killed every plant it touched. "It's still a substantial loss."

Then the phone rang. Horace answered it, walking briskly away into the formal living room where the Leylands never sat, never lounged, and which they had only used once in their twenty years in the house, when entertaining a visiting member of the Jamaican Parliament who later became Prime Minister.

When Horace came trudging back into the room with the heavy, sombre tread of a condemned man's last walk to the gallows, Matilda knew the news was dreadful. Bracing herself and visibly trembling, she quavered, "What now?"

"Dat was our broker. De offer has been accepted. Already, de stock has jumped ten points. It'll double by tomorrow. He says we'll make at least three hundred million."

"Mercy!" Matilda screamed.

The Chance

EVERARD Anderson, a middle-aged black Jamaican, was sitting behind his ornate mahogany desk on the sixty-fifth floor of the Chicago home office when he got a phone call saying that his father had died that morning in Port Antonio. The call came from Uncle Alfie, the youngest of his father's four brothers and the only one now left.

After discussing the funeral arrangements, Everard hung up and sat very still, looking like a man having difficulty digesting a heavy meal.

His father had been in his eighties and lately in bad health, and Everard, an only child, hadn't seen him in years. But it was still grotesque to think that the old man had actually died and would never again walk this earth, and the enormity of that idea caused Everard to slump dispiritedly at the mahogany desk, his head propped up mournfully on his hands.

That night, when he got home, he broke the news to his wife, Beatrice. She had met Everard's father only once, many years previously. Still, she was sympathetic and offered to withdraw from that night's bridge group with neighbourhood women and sit with him in his time of grief.

It was all right, Everard mumbled. He would be fine by himself. He would make his reservations for Jamaica, leave the next day for the funeral and return on Sunday. She did not have to go with him, either, for if she did, she'd probably lose her part-time job, which she had only recently got and really liked.

They ate dinner in the complacent silence that often attends the intimate moments of the long married.

At eight, Beatrice left for bridge. Everard phoned and booked his ticket to Jamaica, took a hot bath and, as he watched baseball on television, thought about his father.

He watched the game drowsily in a huge, lavishly decorated den, conspicuously bedecked with still-life paintings, knick-knacks, crown moulding, leather furniture and faux-finished walls, which made the room look rich and laden with treasures. His father had never been in this room, had never even seen his son's palatial house, an opulent structure of brick and creamy concrete that posed elegantly at the end of a smooth cement driveway and loomed three storeys above the manicured street, its outer walls lapped by an immaculate lawn. All around it, up and down the street, were similar houses – big and fat and conspicuous, with overarching gables like snootily raised eyebrows.

Everard sighed in the sumptuous room, and over the prattle of the baseball game the sound was as plaintive and lonely as a distant foghorn. He wished he and his father had been closer and had not drifted apart over the years. He wished many other impossible things that people always wish for when a loved one dies.

Everard was a practical man, not given much to philosophical musing and seldom swept away by fantasy. Like many Jamaicans, his whole aim in life was to work hard for material betterment. It was the primary lesson he had taught his three sons, now long gone from his household and settled in their own life orbits.

Life was a road, and he had travelled far on it to undreamed-of places. He had come a long way from the small village in the hills of Port Antonio where his father had lived and died, with its ramshackle cottages, its one-room shanties clinging to the mountain slopes, its roadside shops with their gaping, crooked doorways.

And he was where he was all because of a chance meeting he'd had forty years ago on the footpath leading through the village commons. It was the day he ran into Brooker Little.

Everard was sixteen, and his father had sent him into the bush to drive a herd of goats to a new grazing pasture. He was following the footpath that threaded across the grassland of the village commons to the pastures when he met Brooker Little, who was wandering around looking lost.

Brooker was village born and raised, but a long time ago he had gone away to work on a tourist ocean liner, returning to the district only rarely to visit his widowed mother and brag about his world travels. When Brooker showed up on his infrequent visits, he dressed gaudily, as though it was Christmas, grinned often to show off his six gold teeth and smelled vaguely of foreign scents.

Villagers whispered about him behind his back, but said nothing to his face because he was known for his savage temper.

"Everard," Brooker greeted him abruptly, "you see Hector?"

Hector was a village boy with whom Everard had attended grammar school.

"No, Brooker," he replied politely. "You want Hector?"

"I have a job aboard me ship for somebody, and I promise to give it to him."

"Give me de job, Brooker," Everard blurted out in a pleading voice.

He did not know why he said that, the words had just tumbled out of him impulsively, shocking him with his own forwardness. But he suddenly felt that something miraculous was happening, that even the fringing trees and bushes lining the trail were sensing the importance of the moment and straining to eavesdrop.

Brooker looked him over slowly and insolently as if he was examining a donkey for sale. Everard lowered his eyes and gazed meekly at the footpath where it snaked through a grove of trees and disappeared into the woodland.

Finally, Brooker snapped, "You'll have to give me half you pay under de table for a full year."

"Yes, Brooker."

Brooker paused as if thinking. He cleared his throat. "And quarter for de year after dat."

"Yes, Brooker. Whatever you say."

Again came the long measuring look and then, with a snap of finality, like a lizard snatching a fly, Brooker made his decision. "Dis must be only between you and me," he hissed. "Don't tell anybody else."

"Yes, Brooker. I won't tell a single soul, not even me daddy."

In a flurry, Brooker got him his papers and secured his employment, and Everard was swept up from the small village to work as a busboy aboard the cruise ship.

The hard years that followed were at first unremittingly bleak, being mainly filled with toil, weariness and tedium. Everard lived like a rabbit in a crowded warren, sleeping eight men to a cramped, windowless room, occupying unkempt bunks rotated among the off-duty men. Sometimes days would pass before he saw the sea or the sun, his working hours being spent in the dark, sweaty bowels of the ship among bubbling stockpots, smoky grills and broiling ovens. A year later, he was promoted to waiter.

Yet even after paying Brooker his extortionate cut, Everard was still able gradually to accumulate a nest egg. He made shore contacts, bought a Social Security card and got his residency papers by bribing the friend of a friend.

After his shipboard days were over, he took a shore job, went to night school and married Beatrice. Upon graduation, he was hired by a major corporation, where his Jamaican background exempted him from the worst elements of corporate racism by entitling him to the forgiving status of a black foreigner, and with race riots breaking out in the inner cities and the winds of affirmative action gusting across the country, he was swept upwards, like a breakaway kite. During the tumultuous sixties and seventies, whenever racist accusations were levelled against his company, he was hurriedly transferred to the trouble spot and displayed like a flag.

In the wake of his ascent within the corporation came the fatter and fatter houses, the luxury cars, the six-figure income. It was during these busy years that he grew apart from his father and a gulf opened between them.

He sighed again and wondered where the years had flown. Then he fell asleep with the television still on.

Beatrice came home to find him where he usually was in the late evenings, sprawled out on the leather sofa, snoring. She did not turn the television off or disturb the room in any way, for fear of awakening him. She simply tiptoed past her sleeping husband and went to bed.

The next day Everard flew to Kingston, rented a car and drove to Port Antonio. He took the junction road, which snaked a precipitous route over the mountains, and the lush green landscape of his early memories unfolded before his eyes like a familiar picture book from childhood. He drove slowly, pausing to savour scenes that once he had been used to but which now appeared to him, with the perspective of distance and absence, as excitingly exotic. Every now and again he felt like stopping and taking a picture, but then he would immediately chide himself for behaving like a tourist.

Feeling as though he was back in the bosom of a long lost love, he made his way across the mountains and onto the twisty coastal road, which took him to Port Antonio, while the blue-green ocean, nicked by whitecaps, tossed restlessly over his left shoulder in the evening breeze.

Eventually he found his way to Uncle Alfie's house, which sat alone atop a knoll and overlooked a dense slab of mountain land, and he parked on the marl road that encircled the squat concrete bungalow like a lasso, lashing it to the hilltop.

They were waiting for him, his Uncle Alfie and Aunt Petunia, and they acted as though they knew him, and he behaved the same way but did not really know them. They both looked smaller than he remembered. His uncle in particular seemed as if he had shrunk.

Their cottage was so sparsely decorated it looked gutted. On separate walls hung formal graduation pictures of each of their three sons, all of whom now resided in England, dressed in gown and mortarboard and staring off to the side with a ceremonial grimness. From another wall Jesus, his exposed heart mangled with thorns, suspiciously tracked with his eyes anyone passing through the room. Near the ceiling a small green lizard clung upside down to the wall, peering down at them.

As they ate dinner, the country night settled over the mountain range with such a boundless immensity that it seemed as if all the earth itself had been swallowed up in a bottomless belly. Afterwards, with the lights from the small house bravely hollowing out a cavern of gauzy illumination in the pitch-black darkness, they huddled on the veranda, talking. But soon they found themselves harping back to the only thing they had in common, his dead father.

Whenever a moment of silence intruded on the conversation, the background clamour from the overgrown hillside came pouring onto the veranda in a floodtide of rattling and piping made by croaking lizards, whistling frogs, crickets and cicadas.

It was barely nine o'clock when they went to bed. Their talk had been circling helplessly and had now come back to roost on the cousins in England and how they were doing. Everard had not seen them for forty years and kept mixing their names up, only to be gently corrected by his aunt. She suggested he remember their occupations with this mnemonic device: *a*, Anthony was an accountant, *b*, Bedford was a bus driver, and *c*, Cleveland worked as a carpenter.

They were very fortunate, Aunt Petunia added primly, that each of their sons had gone into an occupation with the same initial as his first name. She then carefully recited each son's achievements and the names of their children as though she was reporting on war heroics from the front lines, and Everard had the sorrowful feeling that these two old people, clinging to the hilltop cottage, had been cruelly abandoned. He wondered, with a pang of guilt, whether his own neglected father had felt a similar, woeful abandonment.

He had a difficult time falling asleep, but eventually he did, and when he awoke, the croaking lizards had stopped their maraca rattling and the dawn light, creamy with fog, curled over the land in soft, downy folds like a newborn's hair.

The next day at the mortician's, he found his dead father lacquered and polished in a coffin, dressed in his best suit, his interlaced hands folded neatly across his stomach, looking as formal and stately as a pharaoh. His aunt and uncle commented on how young and alive his father looked, and various mourners who came to view the body claimed to remember Everard as a boy and congratulated him on his obvious success in America.

After the viewing, Everard drove up the hill to the tiny village cemetery to see where his father would be buried, parked his car and strolled towards an open grave a man was digging near the barbed wire fence. He could hear the rhythmic thud of the pickaxe and see clods of dirt flying out between the thick lips of the grave. The cemetery looked overcrowded, the gravestones cluttered together like a tangle of weeds. It was a hot day, and even the mountain top was feeling the scorch of the sun.

Everard was almost to the swollen lip of the grave when a leg bone suddenly spun out of the hole, sailed over the barbed wire fence and plopped into some bushes.

"Hello?" Everard called.

A sweaty black face peeped briefly out of the hole and a voice bellowed, "Everard, is you dat?"

Everard looked hard over the lip of the grave, trying to make out the gravedigger. The man's face was sweaty and grimy from the digging, and his front teeth partly eaten away by jagged cavities. A lifetime of toiling in the hot sun had coarsened his features with a harsh look of premature aging.

"Is Hector, man!" the gravedigger barked impatiently. "You no remember me? We go school together when we was pickney."

"Hector!" Everard said too heartily. "Yes, man! How've you been?"

Hector, standing at the bottom of the grave, was horribly begrimed with dirt and mud. He was panting hard from the exertion and glistening with sweat that streaked rivulets down his dirty face.

"Times hard, Everard," he gasped. "Work scarce. Me have to dig grave for food. What a life for a man o' me age, eh?"

"You looking fit, though, Hector," Everard said lamely.

"Me sorry you daddy dead, Everard," Hector bawled from inside the grave, his voice muffled by dirt.

"Thank you," Everard said, peering down at him.

"You daddy don't want lie beside dis wretch," Hector growled. "You remember dat boasty boy name Brooker Little? Is him dis."

A skull sailed out of the grave and tumbled at Everard's feet, where it wobbled to a stop, grinning as though it had just heard a good joke.

Hector hoisted himself out of the hole carrying pickaxe and shovel, leaned over and took a final, long, appraising look at his workmanship.

"What happen to Brooker?" Everard asked, recoiling from the skull now lying incongruously at his feet.

"Somebody waylay him years ago and bust him head open wid a stone," Hector said bluntly.

He bent down and picked up the skull and showed Everard a welter of spider cracks where shattered bone had been crudely splintered by a vicious blow.

"But who would do a thing like that to Brooker?" Everard cried, wincing at the wound and noticing that all six of Brooker's gold teeth had been extracted.

Hector shrugged and savagely flung the skull over the fence, sending it tumbling in a high, wobbly arc towards a copse of trees, where it landed out of sight with the crunch of a crab shell cracking under shoe leather.

The funeral was held later that afternoon, and after prayers were said and sympathies exchanged, the black-clad mourners drifted off the hillside graveyard in small clumps, leaving Everard and his aunt and uncle alone at the open grave. Hector sat discreetly under the shade of a nearby tree, waiting for the last mourners to depart.

"Well," Aunt Petunia summed up in a small voice, "de journey of life finish for you daddy."

For a few more minutes, they stood silently at the graveside. Late afternoon shadows, dark as old blood, oozed out of the nearby gravestones. Aunt Petunia quietly cried into a frilly handkerchief. Uncle Alfie swallowed repeatedly and kept clearing his throat.

They touched the cold shiny wood of the coffin one last time and shambled away towards the parked rental car, each one shrouded in his own grief. Everard opened the door for his uncle and aunt. As they climbed into the car, he muttered, "I want to say goodbye to Hector."

Crunching over the rough, uneven ground, Everard took a US hundred dollar bill out of his wallet and wadded it in his pocket.

Hector was standing at the graveside, leaning on his shovel, preparing to lower the coffin into the open mouth in the earth. He watched impassively as Everard approached.

"Hector, I wanted to say goodbye."

"You goin' back to America? It look like America treat you good, Everard."

"I can't complain."

"Me was supposed to go to America, too," he said darkly. "Dat dutty boy Brooker Little did promise me. Me glad somebody kill him."

Everard reached hurriedly into his pocket, took out the bill and held it out for him. "I want you to have dis."

A smile of delight lighting up his face when he saw the money, Hector snatched it quickly, as if he was afraid it would be withdrawn, and stuffed it eagerly into a ragged pocket.

"Don't worry, Everard," he said huskily, "me'll cover up you daddy good. No dog will ever dig him up when me done."

"Goodbye, Hector," Everard said, extending his hand. Unused to handshaking, Hector took it limply and gave it a self-conscious little jiggle.

"Dey say everybody get one chance in life, Everard. But me one chance never come. You think it ever goin' come?"

"I'm sure it will," Everard mumbled.

Then he turned abruptly and scurried away to the parked car, feeling like a thief.

The Interpreter

GABRIEL Yap-Sung, a rich cattle-breeder from the district of Pear Tree Grove in St Mary, had no doubt about who he was. Confused Americans could babble in earnest about trying to find themselves, but Gabriel always thought such talk stupid. He was not lost; he knew exactly where he was. He knew what he looked like – a half-Chinese gentleman, pudgy and a little on the short side, with lively, intelligent eyes and a grey, balding head. He knew his own heart and mind. He knew everything about himself.

When he drove through his parish, he was so popular that people, mainly from the lower walks of life, who also knew who he was, would wave. If he had returned every wave he received, he would have been constantly flapping his hands in reply to roadside greetings. So he never waved back but simply stared ahead of him as if in a trance and pretended not to notice.

In spite of this standoffishness, Gabriel still had reason to believe that the common man of the district, the so-called Butu, adored him. Last year at the 4-H fair Butu had voted him the most popular cattle-breeder in the parish. Butu from St Mary were always fawning over him and hanging on to his every word as if he were an East Indian guru.

Gabriel was now in his early sixties with his wife of forty years, Marilee, trailing not far behind. Their four children had disappeared to various continents, leaving the couple alone in the same comfortable family house they had always occupied throughout their long marriage, and where they lived mostly well together.

Yet Gabriel was not happy. With all his wealth a great emptiness still roosted in his belly. Being adored by Butu was like being adored by goats. A man of his years and substance desired more than the adoration of goats. But what? He felt a longing roiling in his belly that his tongue could not utter.

One evening after a couple of rums, Gabriel gazed out at the slumbering land, pleated in dark mountainous folds all around him, smelled a raw emptiness in the cool night breeze and had a revelation wash over him like a crashing wave. What he needed was satellite television. The set he presently owned was capable of receiving only one measly station, JBC from Kingston, whose news programmes hardly ever contained any story of significance beyond Jamaica. Satellite television would give him a ringside seat on international trade disputes, suicide bombings, ambushes, labour actions, political assassinations and Eurodollars. It would expand his horizons, involve him in the world and make him as informed as a city dweller. It would cure him of always feeling so parochial.

The very next day, with great eagerness, Gabriel drove into Kingston and ordered a satellite dish. Two weeks later a crew arrived to install it in his backyard, right next to a leafy pear tree.

When Marilee saw what the workmen were doing and learned that the dish would provide them with two hundred and fifty channels, she begged Gabriel to send the system back.

"Dis is de very kind of thing", she warned solemnly, "dat drive people mad."

"Nobody is going to go mad, woman. We'll just have more TV to watch. Dat's all."

So the dish was put in and turned on, and Gabriel immediately became a fanatical channel jumper. Sitting on the sofa and using the television clicker, he would hop from one programme to the next, sometimes lingering for a few seconds before he darted off to another channel. He reminded Marilee of a hummingbird driven mad by too many blossoms. She got so that she couldn't stand to be in the same room with him when he was doing this annoying channel jumping.

Eventually, Gabriel put aside his flitting ways and settled down to a steady diet of world news. He grew particularly fond of stories that showed belligerent nations in negotiation with each other.

After a month or so of steady television watching, he took on the airs of an expert in international relations and on weekends could be found in a local rum bar holding forth on the squabbles between foreign countries – many of which the villagers had never even heard of.

One midday, as he sat pasted to his chair watching CNN, he noticed something peculiar. Every important man or woman involved in negotiations on the world stage had an interpreter. Usually, the important person would whisper into the ear of the interpreter, who would then relay out loud to the other party what the important person had said.

One night, as Marilee was preparing to retreat to her bedroom to escape the heartbreak of channel jumping, Gabriel said to her, "See dat man standing beside dat woman? He's her interpreter. Watch how she talks. She whispers to her interpreter and he tells everybody what she said. Isn't dat something?"

"Poor soul don't know de language," Marilee murmured sympathetically, squinting at the set.

"No," protested Gabriel, "is because she's important. Only important people have interpreters."

Marilee disagreed. "If she knew the language, she wouldn't need an interpreter."

"I want a interpreter, too," Gabriel said in the voice of a small child hungering for a new tricycle.

Marilee stared with disbelief at her husband.

"An interpreter? Why you need an interpreter? Who you talking to dat don't understand you?"

"Butu."

"Listen, nuh, de hour is late and is time to sleep. Don't mad up me brain with you foolishness."

Then she was gone, closing the bedroom door firmly behind her, marooning Gabriel in front of the television.

Gabriel was used to getting what he wanted. He was richer than many small banks. He owned more cows, more land, more pigs than anyone else in St Mary. In the community he was a genuine Busha – Big Boss – on whom many people depended for their livelihoods. Generations of some whole families in the district had put all the food on their table because of him. If he wanted an interpreter, he would get one. If he looked ridiculous, no one in the parish would dare tell him so to his face.

He decided to make his headman, whose name was George and who had worked for Gabriel since boyhood, his interpreter. George was perfect, being meekly willing to go along with anything Gabriel wanted. Aside from the relationship they had as employer and employee, they attended the same church where

George was widely known for his ecstatic outbursts of speaking in tongues during revival meetings.

"Why de Holy Ghost never call on you, eh?" Marilee whispered to Gabriel one Sunday in church after watching George swoon in another ecstatic trance.

"When de time is ready, he will call," was all Gabriel could mumble lamely in his defence.

George was definitely the right man for the job.

The next day was butchering day and, as was the custom, Gabriel picked up George at the headman's cottage and drove with him to the butchering tree. On the way, Gabriel explained to George about becoming his interpreter.

"So what dat good for, sah?" George wondered with perplexity.

"It's like speaking in tongues," Gabriel said, half-jokingly. "But instead of talking for the Holy Ghost, you talking for me."

"Hmmm," George said.

But he fell in with the game readily, and by the time the two men had reached the butchering tree, they had worked out between them the mechanics of how the interpreter would work.

George thought it was a little peculiar for two grown men to be behaving this way, but Gabriel was his boss and in the past had done other things that seemed stupid but turned out miraculously right. For example, there was the time that Gabriel bought land on an overgrown mountain that didn't even have a road cut to the top. Everyone who knew about the purchase, including George, thought Gabriel was a fool. Two years later bauxite was discovered on the land, increasing its value one hundred times.

So who knew?

The day labourers were waiting for them at the butchering tree, which had a thick, low-lying branch from which a slaughtered cow could be hung by a chain and the carcass dismembered.

George bounded out of the truck wearing an expression of triumph. Before anyone could say a word, he bellowed, "I'm de interpreter for Busha from now until Busha dead! Any word dat come from Busha must come from my mouth!"

The men milled around him with perplexity as if they were being taught the rules of a new game but didn't understand.

Busha whispered to George, "Tell dem good morning on my behalf."

George bawled, "Busha say good morning to the whole lazy lot o' you. Now bring de cow!"

The cow was led by a chain around its neck until it was standing directly under the tree. Gabriel gently pressed the muzzle of his .38 revolver against the short, stiff nap of hair drawn snugly across the forehead of the cow and pulled the trigger. From the distant mountains cracked the sharp whiplash echo of the gunshot across the valley. Without a sound, the cow collapsed instantaneously, tumbled over on its side, kicked twice and was dead.

Soon the cow was hanging bleeding from the branch while the labourers hacked at its joints and muscles until all that was left on the hook was the stumpy, bloody head swinging in the breeze like some hideous modernistic mobile in an avant-garde museum.

Four pick-up trucks driven by regular customers arrived, the newcomers greeting the news about the interpreter with incredulity and staring at Gabriel as if he'd gone mad.

One of the buyers, a literal-minded Kingstonian, stubbornly refused to go along with the pretence. He addressed all his remarks directly to Gabriel and would not listen to any reply that came from George. When Gabriel refused to talk to him directly, the man stomped off saying that this was obviously a human case of mad cow disease.

As the unhappy buyer drove away, the remaining regular customers gloomily milled around the butchering tree under the stern gaze of the dangling, dismembered head, selecting the cuts of meat they wanted and muttering about the strangeness of life in the country.

"Busha must have had a stroke," one man speculated to George, trying to find some sensible explanation that would repair the morning's frontal assault on logic and common sense.

"Yes," George agreed eagerly, thinking that things had already gone so far that even he was beginning to look the fool. A stroke, however, fitted in nicely with the way things were going and absolved him of any responsibility for Gabriel's stupid game.

As for Gabriel, he was feeling global and contemporary, like a character on the World News rather than a puny, myopic resident of Pear Tree Grove. At one point, especially when the stubborn Kingstonian was raising a stink, he'd almost called the whole thing off and dismissed the whole business of the interpreter as a joke. But now he was rather enjoying the charade. It reminded him of the fun he'd had as a child playing make-believe.

A few minutes later everyone went home, trickling across the pastures as the hot noon sun scraped at the land with a coarse rasp of heat that drove even chickens into the shade.

Gabriel had had a stroke that had robbed him of speech and required him to have an interpreter. That was the message the workmen took with them that day to spread throughout the village's rum bars.

Over the next few days, word spread about Gabriel's affliction. People would stop George on the street to ask him if what they had heard about Busha was true, and George would solemnly confirm everything they had heard, adding an extra daub of colour with every telling. He became puffed up with a sense of self-importance and began materializing out of the fog early every morning in Gabriel's front yard so he could accompany him as his interpreter.

Wherever they went, villagers greeted them with unblinking pretence as if there was nothing amiss about a Chinyman Busha, born and raised in the district, suddenly trotting around with his black headman claiming to be his interpreter. Shopkeepers who served them took great pains to direct their questions and remarks to George rather than to Gabriel and waited patiently while the two men huddled and whispered as if translation and discussion were indeed taking place *sotto voce*.

One day Gabriel and George stopped at Miss Woods's grocery, a woebegone stick shack tilting on the muddy fringe of the roadway, to buy a soft drink.

As Miss Woods served them, she glanced at Gabriel and remarked out loud, "Is too much love of money dat cause dis misfortune to catch Busha."

"You hear what dat damn woman say 'bout me?" Gabriel whispered furiously to George.

"Busha say you batty need a wiping," George shot back crisply.

"Whose batty need wiping?" Miss Woods shrieked with outraged horror.

The argument that ensued was nasty and vulgar, and with salvos of earthy insults on the themes of hygiene and genealogy whistling past their ears like bullets from a drive-by shooting, Gabriel and George eventually backed out of the shop, vowing never to return.

What especially irked Gabriel was that this was the same Miss Woods who had always been courteous and respectful to his face and who had once come to him seeking a loan to tide her over bad times. Gabriel had lent her the money and, as borrowers often do, she had practically grovelled before him in gratitude. Now she was openly scornful as she chased the two men out of her rat-trap shop.

That was only the beginning. The same thing began happening more and more often and wherever Gabriel travelled throughout the district of Pear Tree Grove. Now that people thought he did not understand them, they openly discussed his fate and reputation right in front of him, calling him "stingy", "hard-hearted", "conniving", "money-loving", "backslider", after warning George not to translate. One woman tartly said that she always knew that sooner or later life would catch up with Busha and make him pay for his sins.

Another villager, still seething over the real estate transaction in which Gabriel had got the better of him, chortled out loud the first time he saw Gabriel and his interpreter together.

"Serve him right," the wretch declared brazenly.

Gabriel sank deeper and deeper into gloom.

One night, after a particularly harrowing day of being called to his face every unkind name in the book, Gabriel sat on his veranda, a shadow drawn over him like a mourner's veil, and told Marilee, "I don't even know who I am any more. You should hear what people saying 'bout me. I'm mean. I'm stingy. I don't have a heart. Money is me god. What is dis, oh Lord? Who dese people talking about?"

"Is jealous dey jealous of you," Marilee said.

"I used to think dey adored me."

"Is lie dem used to tell."

Gabriel buried his head in his open palms. "After all I do for dem," he wailed. "To find out dat Butu don't love me!"

"All things are revealed in de long run," Marilee said scripturally. "But no matter what anybody tell me, I know in me heart dat is dat satellite dish start de whole thing."

That night when Marilee was asleep, Gabriel strolled outside into the cool darkness and glanced up at the stars glowing in the bottomless country night. He began to wonder who he was. It was a subject he'd never thought about before, but a mood of sadness and longing was on him so strongly that he began to wonder if he was really him or if, unbeknownst to him, his body had been captured by an alien from another parish. It was a peculiar feeling he felt that night as he looked up at the stars, a feeling so strong and perturbing that he couldn't get it out of his mind. It dawned on him that a man was nothing except how he was seen through the eyes of others. It was a very disturbing thought, and thinking it brought tears to his eyes and made him feel maudlin. Why, he couldn't say. Without the respect of his fellow earth-walkers, a man was nothing but an airborne thistle in the breeze, unloved, uncherished and unmourned when his days came to an end. And that was how Gabriel now felt.

With the enormity of this realization on his mind, he lay in bed wondering who he truly was and listening to the insects baying abroad in the darkness. He felt empty and light and several times thought fearfully that if he did not hold on to the bedsprings, he might float out through the window and be swallowed up by the terrible mouth of the night. The idea haunted him so much that he got out of bed and padded to Marilee's room. He shook her awake and asked her feverishly, "Who am I?"

Marilee blinked at him through a blur of shadows, muttered, "An idiot", rolled over and fell back asleep with a rattling snore.

Gabriel shuffled out of the room.

That Sunday the Yap-Sungs went to church. They went to church for the same reasons they'd always gone to church, because it gave them an opportunity to dress up in their finery, and it was what a country dweller did on a Sunday morning. Without church, Sunday would not seem like Sunday, which would also throw off Monday, ruin Tuesday and discombobulate Wednesday. In fact, the whole week would be undone were it not propped up by the solemn observances of Sunday. Moreover, Sunday services had been the venue of some of the sweetest sleep Gabriel had ever enjoyed.

There was a guest preacher that day, a noisy revivalist of fervent passion who delivered every homily in a bellow. Usually, the more histrionic the homily the quicker Gabriel fell asleep and the sounder he slept. But this Sunday he was uncharacteristically attentive. The preacher was just hitting his stride when Gabriel began to twitch as if he was being attacked by fleas.

"Gabriel, behave yourself!" Marilee hissed.

"Xyycy zxxh spppttt blllaaaat!" Gabriel intoned as if talking in tongues, rolling his eyes and leaping spryly to his feet.

"Where you think you're going?"

"Wherever de Holy Ghost carry me!" Gabriel prophesied, adding another blast of gibberish, "Xxxy spllaattt gruubs annhother kkkk hiiiiiiiissss!"

He stood up and, like a deranged bird, began dancing and hopping to the drumming and singing. Marilee tried to grab him by the leg and draw him back into the pew, but she was too late. He was bobbing towards the aisle where the possessed gathered on Sundays to writhe and babble.

Practically every eye in the church rolled in its socket to stare at the normally unmovable Busha, who usually sat through services wearing the expression of a river stone. Now he was seized by a fit and thrashing about among the throng of ecstatic worshippers like any Butu.

George, who was already among the possessed and raving wildly in tongues, sidled up to Gabriel, both of them wallowing in the frenzy of the spirit.

"Hssst multiple shht guano misissshhhh catttttttttttttt!" Gabriel ranted, writhing around on the floor. Then he added at the top of his lungs, "From dis moment on, all speech restore!"

"Busha can talk again!" a nearby woman shrieked.

"A miracle!" another echoed ecstatically.

"Busha, what about de interpreter?" George whispered.

"Go 'way," Gabriel rasped coarsely, "I don't need a interpreter any more! I catch a miracle!"

"A miracle!" another voice took up the cry, and soon the church was ringing with choruses of that triumphant affirmation.

The Yap-Sungs drove home in an exhausted silence. Nothing was more wearying than a spirited church service. Gabriel had also found out that being the voice box of the Holy Ghost was especially draining.

As the green land blurred past the car's window, Marilee roused herself and remarked, "I hope you weren't making a mockery of God."

"Why? Because de Holy Ghost finally choose me?"

"Why you? Why just now? Why de Holy Ghost never choose you before?"

"God work in mysterious ways," Gabriel replied haughtily.

Marilee wisely let the matter drop, and they made their way home in peace. If her husband had blasphemed and mocked, that was between him and God and none of her business. She stared out of the window and said nothing more on the subject.

Word spread throughout the district about the miracle, and once again Butu began saying nice things to Gabriel to his face and waving at him in the street only to be ignored. Gabriel sold the satellite dish and went back to the narrow and stodgy JBC.

Once again Gabriel knew who he was. Everybody in Pear Tree Grove knew who he was. And so long as Butu acted adoringly towards him, he didn't much care whether or not it was a lie.

Hard Woman

ELIZABETH Grove came to Jamaica from Chicago in 1964, fresh off a bitter divorce from her husband of twenty-two years whom she had caught red-handed having an affair with his young secretary. After the usual legal wrangles and manoeuvres, a sympathetic judge had awarded Elizabeth half her husband's business, the marital home, $250,000 in cash, and alimony of $5,000 a month for life.

Bitter in spite of this big settlement, Elizabeth came to Jamaica on a whim, intending to stay at the most for a week and hoping for nothing more than to regain her peace of mind in an exotic Caribbean setting. At forty-four, she was no longer pretty. Despite a childless marriage, her middle-aged figure had grown pouchy, and constant fretting over the divorce had made her hard-looking and stony.

She landed in Montego Bay on a Sunday afternoon and went immediately to her hotel, which was right on the water, and then for a swim. She had never been anywhere like this on her own before, and it was with a feeling of malicious triumph that she splashed around in the balmy Caribbean that Sunday afternoon while the tropical sunset, in a gaudy, soundless spectacle, lacquered the horizon with colours and tints befitting a glossy tourist brochure.

The next day, after a good night's sleep, she rented a car and took a drive across the northern seacoast road towards Ocho Rios. Even though she had to concentrate hard to stay on the left side of the road, she was exhilarated by her own boldness and felt freer than she ever had in her entire life.

On a desolate stretch of road just outside Falmouth, she came upon a dilapidated masonry building circled by a high cut-stone wall with a For Sale sign on it and was so intrigued by the ancient structure that she stopped to have a look. The owner happened to be on the premises, and he was delighted to show around this foreign lady who seemed rich and interested.

Elizabeth was irresistibly drawn to the building, which whispered to her longings for sheltered interiors. It was dark, grimy and cavernous inside, built of thick cut-stone, and reminded her of a bunker. Yet its joyless ugliness that seemed to greedily wall off its private inner space from the outside world exactly suited her post-divorce gloominess.

She spent over an hour walking the building and the grounds, heady from a surge of excitement at the very possibilities she was contemplating, which made her feel as if, in place of her former subservient self, a powerful new woman was emerging in her old skin.

That night at dinner Elizabeth met the Jamaican assistant manager of the hotel where she was staying. The man had recently returned from years of living abroad and, like many Jamaicans with foreign pretensions, was dripping with scorn for his native island and culture. When Elizabeth mentioned casually to him that she was thinking of buying a building, he advised, with a pose of glib superiority, that she offer half the asking price.

He expounded on higgling, telling her that it was part of the Jamaican way of doing business and although his tone was ridiculing she took his advice to heart, unaware that what he had really been trying to do was to impress the foreigner with how far his newly found cosmopolitanism had removed him from these quaint island customs.

Elizabeth tended to take advice too literally, especially when it was given on subjects about which she herself knew nothing. Indeed, in his divorce petition her estranged husband had complained that she was altogether too willing to plan their lives around the forecast of a local astrologer or the latest titbit from some old wives' tale that she had overheard at the hairdressing parlour. Her husband's lawyers had tried to make the jury understand that Elizabeth suffered from a kind of bull-headed stupidity that had driven her husband to adultery for relief, but all the panel could see was that he had slept with a secretary young enough to be his daughter.

What Elizabeth got that evening from the assistant manager was glib advice that she took seriously. What she entirely missed was the cynical tone.

The next day, determined not to be made a fool of and convinced that she now understood higgling, Elizabeth drove to the building, where she was greeted warmly by the seller. He led her into his office, settled her down in an easy chair with a Tia Maria, and prepped her with small talk while he waited for the serious negotiations to begin.

She interrupted his story about the day a crocodile had chased him on the banks of the Martha Brae River with a bid of half his asking price.

"But you don't offer a man half of what he's asking!" the seller cried in dismay. "Dat's not reasonable!"

After some incidental chitchat, Elizabeth made a show of breaking off negotiations and leaving, which brought the seller running to her car door with a counter offer.

"I've made my offer," she said, still determined to act tough. "You have until tomorrow morning at ten to accept it, or I'll be returning to Chicago."

She put the car in gear and began to back slowly out of the driveway, with the sweating seller, his hand on the car door, following her while unleashing a string of garbled explanations about why he could not possibly sell the building for half his asking price.

The truth was, however, that he had doubled his price for the rich tourist, and her offer of half was exactly what he had hoped to get for the building. She got as far as the gate, when the man suddenly threw his arms up in the air and melodramatically surrendered.

"All right. I hope you're satisfied. I'll sell you my ancestral building, left to me by my father's hands, for half price."

He was hoping that she would be moved to pity by the line "left to me by my father's hands", which he had more or less lifted from a popular ballad about Jamaica, but it had absolutely no effect.

After the papers were signed and Elizabeth had gone, the seller, disappointed at not getting twice as much from a rich tourist woman, confided in an old workman who had been with him for years that she was the hardest woman he'd negotiated with in all his born days. Rock-stone was no harder than her heart. Her blood was like diesel oil. She had as much feeling as a piece of pitch pine.

Don't be fooled by thinking that she was a woman. She was no woman. She was a piece of old tyre iron.

The workman, who was a deacon in the local church and a man of considerable sway in his community, repeated the seller's characterization of Elizabeth to his wife, who happened to be a monstrous chatterbox and a vicious spreader of gossip.

By the time Elizabeth finally moved to Jamaica, some six months later, and took possession of the building, her nickname had taken root throughout the community: Hard Woman.

Elizabeth arrived in Jamaica and settled into her burly bunker, walling herself off from faithless husbands and unpredictable betrayals. Her plan from the start was to turn the building into a dress shop for tourists, and she quickly put it into effect.

She had the outside of the building painted a gaudy yellow and put up an enormous sign which read, Elizabeth's Dress Shop, so that the ancient structure simultaneously became an eyesore and an eye-catching attraction to tourists who had had a surfeit of gazing at scrubby white-sand beaches and wraparound blue sea.

From the beginning, the dress shop flourished, sited as it was on the main coastal road heavily travelled by tourists. Elizabeth sold a simple line of summery dresses, of her own design and manufacture, which quickly caught on with tourists. They saw in them a spanking, exotic quality that was lost on the local eye. Soon the dresses that she was manufacturing in the back of her building with the help of local seamstresses (who knew her reputation and were grimly convinced she was robbing them) began selling so fast that she could not keep up with the demand.

During these first months, Elizabeth was too busy to know anything about the nickname and reputation she had secretly acquired in the community. All that changed early one morning when she overheard two local women gossiping outside her window and discovered to her astonishment that her nickname was Hard Woman and that her character was being likened in whispers to a rusty bar of scrap iron.

Her first impulse was to charge indignantly outside and heatedly deny that she was hard. But her defiant pride stopped her. She would not justify herself to gossips. She was positive, however, that she was not hard. She was merely a foreign woman trying to run a business alone in the Jamaican countryside, where she was constantly besieged by begging, trickery and excuses, and severely handicapped by her own dim understanding of the culture.

Every day she was beset by fresh challenges. She felt that everyone around her was, in one way or another, out to bamboozle her. People who wanted work lied about their skills. Employees tried to cajole her into giving undeserved raises. Outside pieceworkers bawled for higher pay. Suppliers were unreliable. Staff members tried to steal her dress material and had glib ready-made excuses, even when they were caught in the act. Her workers seemed to her to spend as much time idling and chatting as they did working.

In the daily running of the business, she relied on one indispensable word that she used daily: "No". If she said "No" once, she said it at least fifty times every day. But all her no's were necessary and pragmatic no's. None was gratuitous or spiteful. None was, in her opinion, hard.

As the months went by, her reputation for hardness spread and her nickname became her only public identity. People forgot her real name, if they ever knew it, referring to her only as Hard Woman. Meanwhile, Elizabeth became more and more oppressed by the feeling that she was being forced to play-act a part others had scripted.

It was not so much what she did that made her feel this way, but how she was treated. People became guarded and cautious when she had to talk business with them. Workers whom she managed grumbled that she was a slave-driver. Sales clerks in the dress shop seemed to be always whispering conspiratorially and breaking off their furtive chatter whenever she approached.

Strolling outside the walls of her business, she would sometimes hear idlers hissing "Hard Woman" as they loitered just out of reach of the two imposing guards who, armed with four vicious German shepherds, kept the riff-raff at bay.

Elizabeth had made no friends in the district. She knew practically no expatriates and had become close to none of the local women. Her only friendship, and a lukewarm one at that, was with a retired English colonel who ran a nearby waterfront restaurant, had lived in Jamaica for thirty years and was wise to the ways of the local culture. It was to him that she turned for explanations and answers.

One night after dinner Elizabeth told the colonel about her nickname and asked him why she had been singled out for it.

The colonel chuckled good-naturedly. "People here get nicknames based on their nature," he said loftily. "It's an important throwback to slavery days when knowing the nature of this year's overseer could mean the difference between life and death."

"But they named me Hard Woman," Elizabeth protested. "I'm not hard."

"Old negar thinks you are."

"Who're they?"

"The masses. They tell you what and who you are with a nickname."

"They don't know me better than I do. I'm not hard. I don't deserve that name."

The colonel shrugged. "Sometimes it's easier to just become what they think you are," he muttered, sipping a gin and tonic, "rather than to constantly argue."

"What's your nickname?"

"Some of them call me Mr Don't-Care."

"Don't you care?"

"Of course I do. Want another drink?"

"No. I want my real name back. I hate that name Hard Woman."

"What does it matter? Sooner or later we're all dead anyway. Might as well have a drink."

Eight years passed. The business grew bigger, leaving Elizabeth with no time for a social life. She seldom went out except to buy materials and supplies or to check up on outside piece-workers. The only luxury she allowed herself was bird shooting, which she took up on the urging of her friend, the retired English colonel. Her nickname and reputation as a hard woman, meanwhile, had become firmly entrenched in the consciousness of the community and stuck to her everywhere she went, like a stumpy shadow in the noonday blaze.

One night after she'd locked up the store and the back rooms used in the manufacture of her clothes line (she now sold far more than just dresses), a burglar tried to break in through a window, and she fired a barrel of her shotgun at his wavering silhouette. Various Jamaican men of her acquaintance, as well as the colonel, had advised her to do exactly that if her building was ever burglarized: shoot the intruder while he was still outside.

The shotgun blast hurled the thief off the window ledge. He fell with a hideous groan, jumped up and crashed wildly through the bushy backyard, leaving a bloody trail.

Having no telephone, Elizabeth was unable to call the police, and she spent a harrowing night dashing from cavernous room to cavernous room of her stone house with her loaded double-barrelled shotgun, scanning the doors and windows for signs of any more intruders she could shoot while they were still outside.

The next morning the arriving staff found their sleepless mistress red-eyed, armed and jittery. There were lurid scars of a grim shoot-out. One window of the stone building had been blasted out of its frame by the shotgun. A trail of blood dribbled down to the ugly seaweed-strewn beach and then disappeared, leaving the police to conclude that the wounded thief had escaped in a fishing canoe, in which he would most likely die from loss of blood.

Elizabeth was badly shaken by the night-long ordeal. But as she sat in the kitchen, nursing a cup of tea and wondering how on earth she would ever sleep again in this building all by herself, she overheard the detective sergeant praising her for being hard.

By the time the sergeant brought her a statement to sign, she was once again playing the part of a hard woman. Her hands had stopped shaking, and she was so self-possessed that the sergeant was openly admiring.

"I don't think any thief on de island will ever try to break into your house again, missus," the sergeant reassured her.

"Let them come," she replied coolly.

"Lawd Jesus," the awed cook, who had overheard, whispered to the housekeeper.

The housekeeper nodded grimly. "Hard," she hissed.

Some months after the shooting, as she was taking a shower one evening, Elizabeth felt in her left breast an ominous lump, firm and sinister, like an embedded arrowhead. She went to a doctor, who biopsied it. Two weeks later a terse pathology report from

Kingston confirmed the cancer. She hurried to Chicago, where further tests showed that the disease had already spread throughout her bones. She was given three months to live. That night in a hotel room, she wept for the first time since her divorce, throwing herself face down on the bed and sobbing uncontrollably.

She returned to the island, after stockpiling as many painkillers as she could legally transport, and soon was settled once again inside the cool, burly interior of her stone building. She told no one about her condition, although throughout the next few weeks it became apparent to her staff that something was terribly wrong with Hard Woman.

She did not have her usual reservoir of energy. She was losing weight. Even when she was well, she had never encouraged the light-hearted atmosphere found in many Jamaican businesses. But now that she was ill, her wasted presence, flitting through the stone building like an ominous passing shadow, cast a shroud of gloom in her wake.

The pain grew worse. Elizabeth began consuming pills beyond the recommended dosages as the duration of relief they gave grew shorter and shorter. Lashed by excruciating pain, she prowled restlessly between the rows of sewing machines staffed by her workers in the cut-stone bunker. Everyone in the building could see that she was mortally stricken. Rumours flew throughout the district that she was being poisoned. One or two brave souls who worked for her tried to slip in a word of religious comfort and were harshly rebuffed.

Eventually the pain drove her to see a female internist in Falmouth. Shrunken and visibly tormented, Elizabeth sat in the plain waiting room with its crude wooden furniture, thumbing listlessly through last year's greasy dog-eared magazines. She was seen an hour later.

"I need some pain medication," she gasped at the Jamaican doctor, a brown middle-aged woman with a pleasant air of businesslike efficiency. "I have terminal cancer."

Stunned at this bluntness, the doctor was momentarily speechless. Then, to break the ice as she tapped on Elizabeth's back, wincing at the grim, deadened thumps that bespoke cancer, she remarked, "You own the tourist dress shop near that little fishing village outside Falmouth, don't you?"

"Yes. My name is Elizabeth Grove, but no one calls me that. They all call me a nickname. Hard Woman."

"They love to nickname people on this island. They call me Dr Moneybags because I don't give free care. I didn't go to medical school all those years to become a charity worker. I expect them to pay. So I'm Dr Moneybags."

The doctor pressed the glands under Elizabeth's throat, yanking her fingers away quickly as if she'd touched something nasty. She briefly listened to Elizabeth's cancer-riddled lungs and, with a sorrowful sigh, finished the examination and unhooked the stethoscope from her ears.

"I can give you a morphine shot. But it'll cost $250. Morphine is expensive."

Elizabeth stared dully at the dirty tiled floor, thinking.

Every now and again, it suddenly struck her with amazement that she was dying. The thought always made her feel befuddled and confused as if overnight, against her will, she'd been forced into becoming someone else. She sometimes said quietly and repetitively to herself, "Elizabeth Grove is dying," just as a reminder. She did that now while the doctor waited.

"For another $150, I'll add some Demerol. That'll help."

"Dr Moneybags," Elizabeth chuckled mirthlessly, wincing with pain.

"Old negar will rename the world if you let them."

"I hate that name Hard Woman!" Elizabeth cried, bursting into tears suddenly. "I'm not hard! I'm not!"

"No," the doctor murmured sympathetically, giving the poor suffering woman a pat of comfort on her shoulders. "You're not!"

Elizabeth wiped her tears and made a visible effort to control herself. The slump went out of her shoulders as her posture stiffened like a straightening spring. Her face glazed over with a stony look that reminded the doctor of molten lead hardening.

"Take the morphine and Demerol for $400," the doctor urged. "It'll give you some relief."

"I'll give you $200 for both."

"You must be mad!" the doctor yelped. "That's half!"

Beside herself with indignation, she added, "What a hard woman!"

Elizabeth died alone in her stone building the following week.

As she had prearranged, her body was picked up by a local mortician and shipped abroad for cremation, her ashes being returned to Jamaica to be scattered along the mangrove-littered shoreline behind the stone building.

The colonel and an Anglican priest who had been prepaid to do the job attended the ceremony to scatter the ashes. They were accompanied by a handful of the dress shop's former employees, who peeped out glumly from the shade of the mangroves like disgruntled spectators whose team had just lost a drawn-out cricket match. Eventually, the service was concluded and everyone shuffled away from the scruffy beach as if ashamed to have taken part in some public tomfoolery.

With Elizabeth gone, her staff split into feuding factions, and business soon dried up without leadership. Months later the stone building was padlocked by the police to prevent unlawful trespass by vagrants.

One evening as the sun set and the sky was grey and heavy with dowdy moth-dust, two old women were trundling past the dark, locked-up building, still gaudy with its huge sign: Elizabeth's Dress Shop. One of them glanced nervously at its boarded-up windows and murmured, "She still inside dere."

"Who?" asked the other, startled.

"Hard Woman," the other replied. "Me no believe she dead."

"Oh no?"

"She too hard fe just dead so."

"You know her?"

"Lawd Jesus!" the other bawled. "Know her? If me know her?"

She drew a gulp of evening air, rich with the scents of saltwater and old skulking mangroves, and began a tangled tale of bygone days when she did piece-work for Hard Woman. The truth was she herself had never worked for Hard Woman, although her neighbour's auntie had.

But the road ahead of them was long and needed a story to shorten it, for the darkness splotching the land was enough to make two old women alone shiver.

The Big Picture

ON the day he was due to take the oath of citizenship, Chester Johnson woke up thinking that he really didn't want to become an American but would rather remain a Jamaican as he'd been born and raised.

It was early Monday morning in Los Angeles. The sun had not yet come up, and the light that fell against his bedroom window was drawn tight, like a rubber band, the darkness stretched thin by the rising sun. Chester lay in bed brooding about the naturalization ceremony that in a few hours would re-make him into an American.

He was alone in his bungalow. Delores had abruptly decided not to sleep over and had got up in the middle of the night and gone home. On the empty side of his bed he could see the outline of her body still impressed on the rumpled sheets in delicate ridges like a footprint on the soft dust of the moon. Outside, the streets were still grainy with the ashes of night and every house still curled up in a rind of sleep and darkness.

Chester got up out of bed slowly. He was a little brown man who lived his life at a turtle's pace, deliberate and slow but with steady gains, and now at forty-five he owned a home, a car and had money in the bank. Nothing in life had ever come easy for him, nor did he expect it to.

He ate breakfast at a small wooden table in a kitchen as stark and serviceable as a bedpan. No decorative touches or whimsical magnets on the door of the refrigerator brightened its sparseness. Delores had tried to soften its austere look but, as a part-time housemate who had her own home to keep up, she could only do so much, especially as Chester stubbornly clung to his threadbare lifestyle.

Thinking about the ceremony ahead had put Chester in a peevish mood. Today he was becoming a citizen to please one Alton Coombs, the new owner of the company where Chester had worked as a sign-painter for the past fifteen years.

Coombs, a burly black American, had fought in Vietnam. About a year ago, shortly after buying the company, he had summoned Chester to his office.

"Johnson," Coombs said as soon as Chester was seated, "I've been going over your personnel file. You've been living here now for thirty years and you're still not a citizen. How come?"

Chester squirmed and mumbled, "I'm Jamaican."

"So we're good enough to feed you but not good enough for you to join us?"

"No, sah," Chester replied gravely. Then he added: "Nobody feeds me. I feed myself."

A long silence followed during which Chester felt his employer's probing stare crawling over his face like foraging ants. Finally, Coombs stood up.

"The reports say you're a good worker, Johnson," he said brusquely. "I want to keep you. But I also like to work alongside men I can trust, men I would like to have at my side in the foxhole. You follow me?"

Chester was a little befuddled at first and was about to ask for an explanation as to why his boss would ever be in a hole made by a fox when he bit his tongue and nodded, "Yes, sah."

"I have high moral standards, and I expect my employees to uphold them, too. You need to swear allegiance to the country that's feeding you. You understand me?"

"Yes, sah."

"Good. Get it done before the end of the year. Deal?"

"Yes, sah."

They shook hands and Chester walked out of the room feeling as if he'd survived a drive-by shooting.

"Damn Americans," Chester muttered as he walked back to the paint shop.

That evening he stopped by the house of his Uncle Ned for advice. Uncle Ned was in a wheelchair and housebound, but he understood Americans better than anyone Chester knew.

"Why does it matter to dis man if I become a citizen or not?" Chester griped. "I do my work."

"I'm sure you do," Uncle Ned said. "But he sees you in de big picture."

"What big picture?"

"Take me, for example. I'm in a wheelchair because of a truck accident I had during the Korean War. I was hauling some hogs to slaughter. I picked up a pretty little woman hitchhiker and she started fooling wid my zipper as I was driving. I got so excited I run the truck into a ditch and broke my back. She took off. Now when I'm dealing wid a brother West Indian, I just tell de true story and we have a good laugh. But when I'm dealing wid an American, I just tell dem I got a war injury, and dey treat me better. I don't tell dem it happened on a Pennsylvania turnpike because I picked up a hitchhiker against regulations."

"But what does dat have to do wid de big picture?" Chester wondered.

"In de big picture, dey see me as a war hero who gave his legs for his country. Wid dem, everything is part of de big picture. Wid us, we meet a man in a wheelchair and if we like him, we treat him good. If we think he's a dog, we treat him like a dog. But we don't have no big picture telling us whether we should treat a man like a man or a dog. We gotta find out for ourselves."

Chester moaned, "Look at dese worries on me head now."

"You see, my boy, you made a mistake. When Americans ask you a big picture question, you gotta give a big picture answer. If dey ask you, 'Why'd you come to dis country?' you can't say, 'To get a job,' even if dat's de truth. You gotta say 'I come here 'cause I wanna be free.' And you gotta say dat even if you were free before you come here."

"What am I going to do, Uncle Ned?"

"You got no choice, boy. De man's got you in de big picture. You gotta naturalize or find another job."

So Chester filed his citizenship application and waited while the paperwork oozed through the serpentine gut of the Immigration and Naturalization Service.

Months and much rigmarole passed. He bought a book on the citizenship test and studied it the only way he knew how, by memorizing every page. Night after night, he sat in his drawing room, swotting the book like a schoolboy.

A couple of months later, Chester was called into the INS office for an interview. His interviewer was a glum Asian, and the questions he asked were disappointingly simple: How many justices sat on the Supreme Court? How many US Senators were there? Could he name one of the freedoms guaranteed by the Bill of Rights?

"Ask me harder questions," Chester urged. "I memorize de whole damn book."

"Take these forms to the cashier," the official said coldly, "and she'll tell you what to do next."

"Ask me a hard question about de Constitution, please," Chester was pleading with the cashier a few minutes later. "Any question you can think of."

The woman glanced at him warily.

"I don't ask the questions," she said, scowling. "My job is to update files in the system."

Chester trudged out of the crowded office, pushing his way through the huddled masses of applicants who milled about looking as dishevelled and grubby as rioters on a television news report.

"Damn Americans," he muttered under his breath as he left the building.

Three months slipped past until finally this particular Monday arrived.

Wearing his Sunday clothes, Chester took his place in a line of other immigrants trooping through the doorway of a cavernous auditorium, variously used for the Shrine circus and other popular events such as the annual tractor-pull. The immigrants, murmuring in a dozen tongues, shuffled past a sign that instructed them to throw their green cards into a barrel. When it was his turn, Chester flipped the shiny plastic card into the open bin, adding his to the hundreds of tiny faces peering up at the enormous ceiling through a bureaucratic glaze.

Forty-five minutes later, after the presiding judge had wrapped up a long-winded speech, seven hundred and fifty immigrants shuffled to their feet with a raspy scraping of leather soles on concrete flooring, raised their right hands and recited the citizenship oath in a mangled chorus of guttural accents that sounded like the simultaneous death rattle from a hundred throats.

Chester was an American citizen.

He woke up the next morning feeling oddly global. His head felt funny. He thought he must have slept badly or perhaps something he'd eaten didn't agree with him, so he sat at the breakfast table and hung his head between his knees to encourage blood to flow to the brain.

He found his mind running on such subjects as Korea and Saudi Arabia, places he could not even have located on a globe but which all of a sudden now seemed more important to him than Mrs Gonzalez, his next-door neighbour of some fifteen years. On his way to work, he fretted about funny things, like the separation of Church and State, the possible bankruptcy of Social Security and the pornographic content of rap music.

Later that day he caught himself parroting rubbish. He was breaking in a boy from Trinidad, who was talking about the hard life he'd lived. Chester looked at him with a solemn face and declared, "You can become anything you want to be."

"I want to become an opera tenor," the boy said sarcastically, "but I can't sing worth a shit. How can I become one?"

"Opportunity lies around every corner," Chester said lamely.

What on earth was happening to him? His head didn't feel right and hadn't since the ceremony. He began burping up bromides and gassy adages. He spent hours cleaning parts of the house that most people never saw and could not possibly know were dirty. Baseboards, chair rails and the tops of window mouldings were scrubbed clean so he could brag about it afterwards.

He began to whine like a housebroken puppy with a full bladder. Every day he had something new to gripe about – the electric bill, the tiny pothole in front of his house, the racket made by the early morning garbage pick-up of a nearby school dumpster, the flight pattern of jets heading for the LAX airport.

He came home one evening after grocery shopping, complaining that all the hot dogs he could find came in packages of ten, the buns in packages of eight.

Delores didn't believe him. "You just buy de wrong package," she said, uncaring.

He insisted that he hadn't, that it was a flaw in the system: ten hot dogs to each package, but only eight buns. The government should be informed about the mismatch.

"Are you mad?" Delores snapped. "You going to report dis to de government? What kind of Jamaican would do something like dat?"

He said he was going back to the store to verify his suspicions.

"Me hungry!" she wailed.

"Eat a peanut butter and jelly sandwich!" he shouted from the garage. "I'll cook when I come back."

"Eat a what?" she shrieked indignantly.

He returned half an hour later, brimming with eagerness to report that there was definitely a mismatch between the packaging of hot dogs and buns.

Delores was gone.

She had made a peanut butter and jelly sandwich, half-chewed it and smashed the bolus against the kitchen wall where it stuck, leaking a brown fluid, like a cracked cockroach .

"Stick this up your rectum," she'd written on a scrap of paper left on the kitchen table. A non-professional would have written "ass", Chester noted, but not Delores: being a veteran nurse, she was a stickler for accurate anatomical terminology. For her, the right word was definitely *rectum.*

But although the change in him appalled his few friends, it endeared Chester to Coombs, who immediately noticed his new attitude.

"That's the spirit!" he said to Chester one night when he found him alone in the shop, standing atop a ladder painting a logo on the trailer of a semi-truck. Chester mumbled some vague nonsense about the only job worth doing was a job well done, which caused his boss to beam from ear to ear.

"You know, Johnson," he said generously, "I'd be in favour of immigration if more like you came to this country."

A week later Chester was promoted to the head of the sign-painting department. A month after that Coombs dropped dead from a stroke. Six months later, Coombs's widow sold the business to a bearded white man, a former draft dodger and aging hippie who had made a fortune from inventing a bloody video game.

The new owner made it plain in his first address to the assembled workers that he didn't care who beat his wife or who smoked pot or who slept with whom so long as the work got done on time.

A few days later Chester was summoned to the new owner's office.

"It looks like you're doing so-so, Johnson," he said stonily, glancing over Chester's personnel file. "But I see that you recently became a naturalized citizen. Why did you do that?"

Noticing with a stab of fear that the company payroll cheque-book lay open on the new boss's desk, Chester shrugged as if he didn't know.

The new owner lit a cigarette and stared probingly at Chester.

"I like a man who sticks to his convictions," he said crisply. "During the Vietnam War, I had to run to Canada to avoid being drafted because I thought the war was wrong. But I never deserted my country by becoming a Canadian. I kept my citizenship and when I received amnesty, I came back. I like a man who stays loyal during rough times. I hate a turncoat."

Chester sat as motionless as a stalked rabbit, suddenly aware that once again he was being entangled in the big picture, that telling the petty truth about why he'd naturalized – to keep his job – would be fatal.

He took a deep breath, stood up and glowered defiantly at his boss.

"I naturalized because I want to be free. I want my child to have de chance of becoming president just like yours."

"I have no children," the new boss snapped.

"Neither do I. But I'm still young enough to. And when my children come, dey'll be free like me. And if you or anybody else don't like dat, you can stick it up your ..."

"My what?"

"Your ass!"

For a tense moment he and the new boss locked eyes with mutual loathing.

"Or," spat Chester a few seconds later, "if you prefer, your rectum!"

"Rectum" made the new boss explode in a loud guffaw. He stubbed out his cigarette and closed the giant chequebook.

"Watch your step, Johnson," he said with grudging respect. "Your kid's not president yet. You may go."

When Chester returned to the paint shop, the Trinidadian boy hurried to his side.

"Dere's a story going round dat de new boss is going to fire you," the boy whispered furtively.

"He was going to, until I showed him de big picture."

"What big picture?"

"I'll explain it to you later. Meanwhile, let's get back to work."

And the two immigrants went back to work.

The Cultivator Who Lost His Heart

A cultivator named Alcott Jones lost his heart one morning somewhere in the commons of the district marked on the maps as The Land of Look Behind. Napping in the shade of a guinep tree when it happened, he woke up unaware of his loss, and at least a day passed before he realized that his heart was missing.

Alcott Jones was not an important man anywhere, not in the district, the parish nor the island. Like many other men he was loved mainly by one person, his wife, Veronica, to whom his continued existence mattered deeply. His adult children, all of whom lived abroad, also loved him, but in the wistful way that aging seafarers loved their old sailing vessels.

So the loss of his heart, though a profound blow to Alcott Jones, had no visible effect on the world, which continued in its same heedless ways as if nothing was different.

Veronica, however, noticed. She could not feel the emptiness in his chest even though she knew her husband of forty years as intimately as a fussy woman knows a favourite old shoe, but she had noticed that his manner had changed for the worse.

"Alcott," she asked one afternoon as they were taking tea on the kitchen step, "what happen to you?"

Alcott Jones was briefly silent before he said, "I lose me heart. It fall outa me chest somewhere in de commons and me can't find it."

"We going have to find it," Veronica said decisively, "no matter how long it take."

"You talk like is something dat happen every day," Alcott grumped.

"Never mind how me talk," Veronica replied sharply. "We need to find you heart before rat or mongoose eat it."

For the rest of the afternoon, Alcott and Veronica combed the commons, looking for the lost heart. By the end of five hours of fruitless searching, Veronica was beating the bushes with a stick and clucking, "Here, heartie! Here, heartie, heartie!" as though she was calling a lost chicken.

Alcott Jones shushed her by asking sarcastically if she expected his heart to come running to her in reply to her idiotic clucking. Veronica, deeply hurt, mumbled defensively that she was only trying to pass pleasantly the hours of searching the thick guinea grass in the hot sun, and please to leave her alone.

They were in the middle of this spat when they bucked up Auntie Matty, checking on her old cow that she left tied up in the commons.

Auntie Matty had lived all her eighty years in the district. During her lifetime she had seen flood, fire and drought, young men die and old men go mad. She knew murder, abandonment and chigger toe. As the local midwife, she had delivered much of the population. Everyone in the district loved her, and there wasn't a family here whose life she had not touched.

"I'll organize some of de old women," she declared when she heard about the lost heart. "If de heart is around, dey will find it."

"I going get some young boy to do a search," Veronica said.

Auntie Matty did not say what she was thinking, that it was no use asking the youth of today to find anything, much less a heart, they were so irresponsible. Instead, she lumbered to her feet, unpleating her old body as if it was a matron's shop-worn Sunday fan, and mumbled, "Well, to each his own order."

Nothing much had happened lately in the district of Look Behind. No one had died recently. As far as anyone could tell, no one appeared likely to die any time soon. Only one woman was pregnant, and she was not due for another seven months. Unlike Kingston with its daily murders and constant turmoil, no one had been murdered here for the past five years, with the result that many of the young regarded the district as hopelessly backward and dull.

So the following week when Veronica called for young boys to join a hunting party for a lost heart, some fifty or so idle youths with nothing better to do showed up in the village square. It was a Saturday, and the group fanned out and swarmed over the commons in a line, watching their footfalls carefully lest they accidentally stepped on the missing heart and mashed it.

For the first hour there was much excited chitter-chatter among the boys as they scrambled over the hillside in a frolicsome mood. But then the sun got hot and the chatter died down as the matted undergrowth of the bush land unfurled ahead of them with a prickly denseness that made even walking difficult.

By the third hour many of the boys were beginning to get bored when one searcher found a lost dream discarded next to the trunk of a star-apple tree. The dream was as limp and soggy as a dead jellyfish, and pieces of it broke off in the hands of a boy who tried to pick it up. A small knot of the youths gathered around, poking at the dream with sticks and making fun of it. Everyone was mystified about its owner until one boy recognized the dream as belonging to a teen who had moved to Kingston to live with his mother, only to be murdered in a drive-by shooting on the day of his arrival.

Veronica came over to see what the boys were gawking at, found them playing with the lost dream and shooed them back to the search after scolding them for being so easily distracted. The youths unravelled over the hillside, and the search continued half-heartedly.

Soon they found scraps from other lives – a discarded ambition rotting under the fraying umbrella of a mushroom; a lost love strewn about in a sandy gully; someone's imagination dangling from the branch of a flame heart tree like a tattered kite.

However, there was no sign of the missing heart, and when the sun set and the youths began dripping off the mountain in globs of two and three, a nagging air of disappointment hung over them, as burdensome and unsettling as the consciousness of original sin to the believer.

The next Saturday, with much noise and fanfare, Auntie Matty launched her search party of some seventy old women who dwelled on the slopes of the surrounding mountains. The women assembled in the square with all the exhilaration and eagerness of participants setting out on a scavenger hunt. It didn't matter to them which part of Alcott Jones they were looking for, whether it was his heart or his batty, just so long as they could mingle out-doors in the fresh air and have fun.

Auntie Matty installed herself at the head of a column with the dignity of a bwana in an African safari movie, and the ragged troop of women scrabbled up the hillside and into the commons, chatting merrily about the latest outrageous rude-boy antics as they began their search for Alcott Jones's heart.

One woman had brought along a bottle of rum, which she passed around liberally, and several of the searchers quickly got drunk. Two old widows fell out over a boyfriend they had shared some fifty years previously, and there was a great deal of shrieking and name-calling as each told her own bitter version of the same story. Auntie Matty tried to impose discipline on the group, but it was too late, a second bottle of rum having been produced and passed around until it was empty. The pseudo safari had by then dissolved into clumps of three or four women who sat chatting in small deep puddles of shadows cast by the stumpy bushes. A few fell asleep after the long hike up the hillside, and many were heard to mutter defiantly that they didn't give a poop about Alcott Jones and his heart, and for all they cared, he could go drown himself in the river.

Just before the final woman straggled off the hillside at sunset, a small party of them stumbled upon a heart and screamed ecstatically for Auntie Matty, thinking that they had proven once again that woman was man's superior. But when Auntie Matty and some of the other elders checked out the find, they discovered that it was an old broken heart dating back to the forties and belonging to a coolie woman who had long ago migrated to Canada, where she had died.

Disgusted, the women dribbled down the hillside, rolled along the narrow marl road that drooled mud over the plywood skirting of the ramshackle shops in the village during the rainy season and disappeared into frail bird-nest shacks atilt on the surrounding slopes.

Alcott Jones still had not found his heart.

Without a heart, Alcott Jones began to think in mad, new ways. One evening as he sat on the grassy slope and gazed at his flock of peaceful goats, feeling estranged from everything he had formerly held dear, it occurred to Alcott Jones that all who lived under the sun were blood relatives dwelling in a kingdom of nothing. It was a dismal thought and not the sort of idle speculation he would normally engage in, but it struck him rather forcefully and kept him awake all the following night.

Having no heart, he suddenly saw no difference between love and hate, sadness and merriment, disappointment and exultation. To his new way of thinking, all the vast and numberless events, doctrines, philosophies and histories – the whole nameable and unnameable galaxy of things seen and unseen, heard and unheard, dead or undead that make up this life – amounted to nothing.

This new thinking wore him down and made him stoop like a man much older than fifty-eight, as if he carried a huge, invisible rock-stone on his head.

One night Veronica sat up in bed shivering, with the bedspread drawn up to her neck, deeply troubled over her mix-up mix-up husband.

"Alcott," she pressed, touching him gently on the bare arm, "me 'fraid."

He did not answer.

The dark countryside stroked them with a mixture of night breeze, cool starlight and the scents of unseen wild flowers. Veronica inhaled deeply as if she was drinking darkness; Alcott burrowed under the spread. He felt the same brush of night that she did but, without a heart, it aroused in him no joy or exultancy.

As Alcott Jones fell asleep, Veronica stayed awake in the lacy light of an old moon and fretted.

For the next few weeks, Alcott Jones was seen throughout the district, walking and talking like a man who was asleep. His face was a painted stone, and his movements looked as though they had been rehearsed. He did little work in his pastures but spent most of his daylight hours sitting, grave and still as a sunning iguana, on the river bank. Residents of the district who came to draw water from the river nodded politely to him but did not linger to exchange small talk. Mothers would not let their small children wander too close to him, and some of the women who always came to that particular stretch of the river to wash their family's clothes chose instead to trudge upstream and find another spot.

Everyone shunned him, from aging men with whom he had romped and played in boyhood, to grandmotherly women who had known and cared for him during his years of helpless infancy.

When he drew near, even his livestock seemed to shy away skittishly. Yet he remained unchanging and emotionless, stumbling his way haltingly along the familiar footpaths of the district, as insensible as rock-stone to the glares he received from onlookers or the bitter muttering his footfalls provoked.

Throughout the Land of Look Behind, the feeling of general uneasiness about Alcott Jones spread. The prevailing opinion was that having no heart he posed a threat to the community. Some people said it was like keeping a domesticated wild animal among them which, though it had attacked no one yet, sooner or later would hunger for prey and devour an innocent. In the church halls some normally sombre heads proposed that a delegation be formed to ask Alcott Jones to leave the district. In the rum bars there was braggadocio talk of chopping up Alcott Jones in public, like a common goat thief. On the streets, on the yam grounds, on the backwoods pastures where only farmers occasionally went, the topic was the same from day to day: what should be done about the man without a heart who prowled among them?

Knowing the strong sentiment running against him, Alcott Jones began feeling more and more cut off from the companions of his youth. The Land of Look Behind had always been his home; he had lived nowhere else, and even now, as a man of fifty-eight years, he had never slept a night in any other bed than his own. Yet he was seriously considering fleeing his birthplace. One day he was wondering where to go when he ran into Auntie Matty.

"Alcott," she said to him brusquely, "two crocodile in de river. One bite you if you try to cross. De other help you across the river. How can you tell dem apart?"

This abrupt questioning made Alcott Jones feel like a schoolboy who was secretly slow at his lessons and whose dimwitted nature was now about to be exposed and ridiculed by the teacher before the entire class. He swallowed his pride with a shrug of surrender. "How?"

"De one dat bite, bite. De one dat help, help."

"Me no understand dis riddle," Alcott Jones muttered crossly.

Auntie Matty tottered unsteadily on the sloping ground.

"I give me own heart away to a boy who went to sea in '49," she said, regaining her footing. "Since den me have no heart, either. No one know but me, and now, you."

"You!" Alcott Jones exclaimed. "Auntie Matty have no heart!"

"Shhhh. Mind man hear you. Listen to me, Alcott Jones. A man with a heart and a man without a heart look de same on de outside. Behave like you have a heart and no one will know de difference."

"Dis come like a parable to me," Alcott Jones griped. "Me no understand parable. Me no understand dem in church, and me nuh understand dem outta church."

"Understanding soon reach you," Auntie Matty chirped.

"Plus", muttered Alcott Jones sullenly, "everywhere 'bout me I see pure nothing."

Auntie Matty glanced around her as if she was sharing a dark secret. "Me see de nothing, too," she whispered, shuffling off. "But me make believe is something."

Alcott Jones stared after her as indignantly as if she had tried to tell him a smutty joke during a church service.

"Treat nothing like something?" he bawled after her. "What kind o' something is dat?"

"Is better dan nothing," she flung over her shoulder before vanishing into the foliage like a duppy.

A few days later a young boy playing in the street stepped on a rusty nail, came down with lockjaw and died. News about the boy, who had been a well-liked, cheerful and obedient child, spread through the district, and around noon a day labourer came rushing into the yam fields to regale Alcott Jones with details of the dreadful story. So moved was the labourer by his own tale that he rashly offered himself up in the boy's place if God was listening and would agree to a swap. God was evidently not listening because nothing was changed by this offer. The boy remained dead, and the yam fields baking in the noonday sun continued to blur the mountainside with rippling cellophane sheets of heat.

Alcott Jones, for his part, showing no sign of sorrow, stood on the old yam ground, looking perplexed. He thought about the boy's death and the labourer's lamentation, his face as blank as a dunce's slate. What did it matter that the boy had died at ten? He would have died eventually, at thirty or sixty or eighty. Why all this lamenting over a few measly years?

Peering up hopefully at the face in front of him, the labourer searched hard for a twitch or even a batted eyelid that signalled, if not sorrow, then at least an ounce of regret over the loss of such a young life. Alcott Jones remained stony and unmoved.

But the labourer was staring at him with such an impassioned intensity that Alcott Jones felt that something, some gesture or remark was called for, although he did not know exactly what. As he stood there, showing a rock-stone face, Alcott Jones suddenly understood the lesson Auntie Matty had tried to teach him with her parable of the two crocodiles.

"I sorry for the boy's family," Alcott Jones mumbled. Then he hung his head as many do when they speak the word "sorry".

"You find you heart, sah!" the labourer exploded with joy, hugging Alcott Jones in a spontaneous expression of delight that nearly toppled them both onto the dirty earth.

The jubilation that followed after that in the Land of Look Behind had more joy and sparkle in it than old-time Christmas.

In no time at all word raced throughout the district that Alcott Jones had found his heart. Suddenly, everywhere he went he was met with wreathing smiles and expressions of congratulations, Look-Behinders greeting him as if he was a Lazarus who had got up and walked away from his deathbed. Veronica wailed with relief and repeatedly gave thanks, and his children sent postcards from overseas, giving words to their gladness.

Alcott Jones, meanwhile, fell in with the spirit of the time and began a deliberate masquerade. He wept at funerals, pretending grief he did not feel. He danced at birthday parties, though he felt no joy at the passing of another year. He voiced regret over accidents and misfortune, and no one knew that behind his sham of caring he felt nothing. Among his fellow cultivators, he wailed with passion over rainstorm, drought, pothole and infestation of chi-chi ants. At church services, he feigned the enthusiasm of the spirit, his face seemingly afire with the glow of the Holy Ghost, even speaking aloud in tongues with gibberish of his own creation. And in all of these demonstrations no one, not even Veronica, could tell that without a heart he was still haunted by the unchanging, everlasting and persistent nothing and pretending it was something.

A few weeks later, as Alcott Jones was in the commons counting his cows, he stumbled on the above-ground roots of an old tree, fell and landed on his face, and found his heart still thumping under a leaf, in the exact place where it had rolled out of his chest many months before.

He took up his heart, brushed the grains of dirt off it and put it back in his chest.

But he told no one.

The Riddle

ALVIN Chambers was a fifty-eight-year-old engineer who owned and ran a wrought-iron business in Brown's Town, St Ann's parish. He and his wife Sylvia had married late in life and had an only child, a daughter they named Cindy. They bought an old great house in a guinea grass field on the outskirts of Brown's Town, where the threesome lived contentedly with the help of two maids and a garden boy.

Alvin fancied himself a profound thinker. He felt that his cast of mind went one of two ways: either he was deep or shallow. When he felt deep, he thought he was profoundly deep; when he felt shallow, he thought he was profoundly shallow. This secret self-appraisal he kept to himself, and for all the world knew, deep or shallow, he was the same Alvin from day to day, unchangeable and solid as rock-stone, a faithful husband and an adoring father.

One evening Alvin was relaxing on his veranda watching the flocks of egrets sailing towards their woodland roosts when Cindy appeared at his elbow, looking troubled.

"Daddy, can I ask you a question?"

Cindy was the kind of child Jamaican teachers called "precocious", meaning gifted but too smart for her own good, and lately she had been peppering Alvin with deep questions that left him feeling as though he'd eaten bad fish: Why was she born? Why must she die? What would happen to her when she died?

These were questions Alvin had dogmatically answered over the past years, drawing on the moral certitudes of his rural Jamaican childhood. You were born to serve God. Dying was the only way to get to heaven. After you died, if you were good, you went to paradise. If you were bad, you went to Kingston. Cindy hated that corny joke.

If he had no good answer, he'd say, "You'll find out some day," which also left Cindy feeling resentful and patronized.

Now that she was about to ask him another question, Alvin steeled himself as though bracing for a thump.

"What?" he asked bravely.

"Why does de chicken cross de road?" she asked solemnly.

"Eh?" Alvin exclaimed. "What kind o' question is dat?"

"It's a riddle for Miss Watkins's class. You know de answer?"

Alvin summoned up a blurry picture of Miss Watkins from the last PTA tea party, a short American white woman in her thirties who wore delicate horn-rimmed glasses perched on the very tip of her nose, like the elegant hood ornament of an expensive English motor car.

He squirmed. "No, I don't know de answer."

Cindy shrugged and mumbled, "Damn! I was hoping you would."

After she was gone, Alvin sighed and seemed to deflate in the chair. He hated disappointing Cindy, but puzzles and riddles tended to cling to him like tapeworms, and deep inside something warned him to keep away from this one. Yet in spite of these misgivings, he muttered softly to himself, "Why *does* de chicken cross de road?"

That night, as they were settling down to sleep, Alvin shared with Sylvia the funny riddle that Cindy was grappling with for Miss Watkins's class.

"What business is it to an American why a Jamaican chicken cross a Jamaican road?" Sylvia asked crossly, weary after a long day at work as an accountant for a sugar factory in Runaway Bay.

"You know why de chicken cross de road?"

"Certainly not! I'm not a chicken."

They settled down to sleep.

Sylvia griped, "Dat woman just come from America and already she trying to drive people mad wid her riddle. I wonder if she's wid de CIA?"

"Why would she be wid de CIA?"

"Spread disinformation, destabilize de government, drive de country mad."

Then she shifted her considerable rump restlessly beside him, causing the bedsprings to squeal like an injured puppy.

A week passed, with the riddle giving Alvin no peace. He was thinking about it constantly.

Before the riddle, when he was idle and his mood deep, his mind used to shuffle through patternless daydreams, like an old man playing solitaire. If his mood was shallow, his mind would recite doggerel he'd had to memorize in English literature classes. Now, as soon as his thinking was not focused on something specific, the riddle popped up in his consciousness like a hideous jack-in-the-box: *Why did the blasted chicken cross the blasted road?*

He thought of various reasons that might send a chicken scurrying across the road – a stalking mongoose, perhaps, or a circling chicken hawk – but none seemed compelling enough to explain the universal road-crossing behaviour of the species. The obvious reasons – to find some food, to get a drink of water – seemed too obvious. It occurred to him that every chicken could very well have its own reason for crossing the road. But, according to Cindy, Miss Watkins had said that she had in mind one particular answer.

Alvin was stumped.

But he was not a man to be stumped without a fight. When he was in university, he once spent a week of eighteen-hour days trying to solve a knotty calculus problem.

He gritted his teeth, put on his thinking cap and tried harder.

One night, with Sylvia berthed at his side and rumbling like a motorboat, Alvin lay abed in a deep mood, reviewing what he knew about the chicken.

Chickens did not cry, did not laugh, did not smile and never looked you straight in the eye. Although his experience with chickens was limited to eating them, he'd always had the impression that they were filthy, brainless birds, doomed to live briefly and then die without a trace, leaving behind nothing but bones, beak, claw and another chicken. Could a life be more meaningless, more pointless?

Indeed, what was a chicken but flesh and bone wrapped into a spherical body in which a primitive spark of consciousness flickered?

It was then that a deep idea clubbed him over the head. Wasn't a man just another spark of consciousness embedded in the same flesh and bone moulded into a different shape? Underneath it all, how was a man materially different from a chicken?

He slid out of bed, padded to the window, stared up at the luminous Milky Way sectioned by the burglar bars and shuddered at that awful, worrisome insight.

Still sleeping, uncaring Sylvia, who was never deep, rolled over and bombarded the room with a thunderous barrage of snores.

The next morning Alvin sat at the breakfast table listlessly playing with a bowl of banana porridge. Sylvia, bustling to get dressed for work, blew through the room and flicked him a glance of concern.

"Alvin, you don't feel well?" she asked.

"I didn't sleep much," he muttered gloomily.

A moment later he asked casually, "Cindy, Miss Watkins give you de answer to de riddle yet?"

Cindy looked up from the schoolbook she was reading. "No. But we should get it soon. We're learning about pragmatism."

Sylvia overheard and yelled from the bedroom, "What kind of foreign foolishness is dat you're studying?"

"Pragmatism is not foolishness!" Cindy yelled back. "It's philosophy."

"Philosophy is foolishness," came the tart reply.

"It is not!" Cindy cried indignantly. "Daddy, tell Mummy dat philosophy isn't foolishness!"

"Philosophy is not foolishness," Alvin mumbled. To Cindy he whispered, "You mother is not a deep person."

Sylvia bawled from the other room, "What you say, Alvin?"

That afternoon Alvin stopped by the small, dingy town library and looked over its modest collection of philosophy books. Most had never been borrowed and had pages as crisp as newly printed bank-notes. An hour later he appeared at the checkout desk with two heavy philosophical tomes, one by a Scotsman, the other by a German.

The librarian, an acquaintance, stamped the due date on the loan flap and carefully handed him the books.

"Philosophy," she murmured respectfully. "Me never know you so deep."

"Plenty people dat think dem know me don't really know de inner me," Alvin sniffed.

"Beg your pardon," she muttered sarcastically.

For the next few days Alvin read philosophy on and off in his office.

The Scotsman said there was no god and there never had been one, that there was no cause for anything, that everything happened randomly and for no reason. The German said that everything was nothing, that life was unreal and had no meaning.

Alvin went from the one to the other, his brain being battered by bombastic speculations. Their words transported him to a strange neighbourhood, an insubstantial world where nothing was as it appeared, where paradox lurked constantly underfoot like a scorpion. It was a deep, topsy-turvy, godless world in which Alvin felt bewildered and lost.

Getting there, moreover, had not been easy. The German could not write a clear sentence if his life depended on it, and the Scotsman was as fun-filled as an aquarium snail. Even worse was that neither addressed the riddle, except by implication. The Scotsman implied that the chicken was propelled by randomness; the German that there was no chicken and no road to cross because it was all a dream.

Alvin emerged periodically from his office, gulping for air. For days, his offhanded remarks to his staff were nonsensical and filled with bizarre allusions to chickens.

Word of his raving soon reached the ears of Sylvia. One night she took him to task on the veranda.

"Why you going on so at work about chickens?" she asked.

"I was speaking philosophically!" Alvin protested.

Sylvia stared at him with an expression of grim shallowness that told Alvin she didn't understand. "Philosophically, my foot! Tomorrow you going to de doctor."

"I'm not going to no doctor. Nothing wrong wid me."

"You going," she repeated emphatically.

The next day they went.

In a small community such as Brown's Town, lives criss-crossed and intersected one another in different phases. Everyone knew everyone else by sight, experience or gossip. The doctor, for example, once shared an ancient rivalry with Alvin when they played cricket against each other as schoolboys on their respective schools' teams. Educated abroad, the doctor had returned to Jamaica ten years previously to establish a flourishing general practice within the city limits.

In a cramped examination room, the doctor first listened patiently to Sylvia's complaint about her husband's ranting about chickens before turning to Alvin and prodding him to speak his heart of hearts openly. Alvin began by explaining, slowly at first but gradually gathering steam, that thinking deep about Miss Watkins's riddle had opened his eyes to a profound insight, that man and chicken shared a common doom.

"Damn CIA," Sylvia fumed.

The doctor shushed her and told Alvin to continue.

Alvin continued. The chicken ended up being eaten by man; the man ended up being eaten by a worm; the worm that ate the man who ate the chicken ended up being eaten by another chicken, which would eventually be eaten by another man. It was a vicious cycle, as bad as dog eat dog, bleak, ugly and depressing.

Just because he was a Jamaican didn't mean that he couldn't think and be philosophical, too. He could think. He could speculate about life and have earthshaking philosophical insights as profound as those of any Scottish or German thinker. And his insight was this – underneath it all, everyone was a chicken.

After Alvin was finished, the doctor sat ominously silent for some heart-stopping minutes. Then he opened his prescription pad and began rapidly scribbling on it.

"What's wrong with Alvin, doctor?" Sylvia asked in a quavering voice.

Absorbed in writing a prescription, the doctor took his time before he said, "He thinks everyone is a chicken."

"I can see dat," snapped Sylvia. "But why?"

The doctor shrugged. "If you need a clinical diagnosis, you can call it chickenitis."

"Chickenitis?" Sylvia gaped. "What is dat, pray?'

"Thinking that everyone is a chicken."

"Now see here ...," Sylvia began indignantly.

"Just follow this treatment," the doctor said, handing her his scribbling.

He cuffed Alvin on the side of the head, said, "Birdbrain, why don't you mind your own business?" and left the room.

"Chickenitis!" Alvin sneered, yelling after the retreating doctor, "You just getting back at me because I clean bowl you for a duck in a Sunlight Cup cricket match forty-two years ago!"

"Stick to wrought iron, you idiot!" the doctor's reply came back faintly from somewhere in the corridor.

Sylvia peered at the scribbled treatment.

"Almighty saviour," she moaned. "Will you look at all dis treatment?"

That night, when Alvin came to bed, he found that Sylvia had hung blankets over the windows to block out starlight.

"What did you do?" he asked.

"It says here ..." She opened the prescription and read, "'No staring at de night sky with awe and wonder.' You been doing dat behind me back?"

"Sometimes," he admitted guiltily.

She read more. "'No reading of deep foreign books.' Where dem two book you get from de library?"

Alvin retrieved the books from under his side of the bed where he had tucked them out of sight. Sylvia sat in a chair and leafed through both books.

"Good Lord," she murmured, "no wonder you think everyone is a chicken."

She put the books carefully down on the bureau as if they might explode.

"From now on, you read only de newspaper."

"Why?"

She glanced at the pad and muttered, "'To restore you to a piddling outlook.'"

"A what?"

That Sunday, dressed in their best finery, the whole family went to church, a thing they usually did only on special holidays such as Easter or Christmas. The minister, who was visiting from Kingston, gave a boring sermon on redemption that put a dozen hardened churchgoing matrons under within minutes. The doctor and his family were also there, dozing in the pew across the aisle, and the two families exchanged sleepy half-hearted waves.

At the end of the service, Alvin wobbled out of the church as if he was drunk. "My God," he gasped, once the three of them were out of earshot of the other groggy worshippers, "he was boring!"

"It's treatment," Sylvia said.

"I don't have chickenitis," Cindy whined. "Why am I getting treatment?"

The treatment had other steps. Alvin was to watch local soap operas on television daily, and to visit rum bars after work three times a week, where he was to chat rubbish.

So every evening as the egrets sluiced through the twilight skies to their woodland roosts, Alvin sat on the veranda, receiving the transfusion of a piddling outlook from the newspaper. Three nights a week he took treatment at the local tavern. And Sundays found him and his family, along with other worshippers, dozing fitfully in the pews during the homily.

This regimen was severe but produced miraculous results. In a matter of days everyone began to remark on the improvement in Alvin. His dogmatism came flooding back along with his God-given Jamaican cockiness. Gone was the raving about chickens. But he was still curious about the answer to the riddle. He decided to pay Miss Watkins a visit.

One lunchtime Alvin drove up to the school, parked his car and plodded his way over the grassless grounds, past knots of students eating and chatting under scraps of shade, making the background buzz of a thousand bees.

He found Miss Watkins in her classroom eating lunch and soon was sitting across from her at a desk defaced by the bruises and nicks of the unruly student generations.

For a long, uncomfortable moment, Alvin stared vacantly at the accumulated scribbles and carvings of hearts, planet Earth and aircraft on the wooden desktop, feeling stupid and wondering why he had come.

Miss Watkins finally broke the silence by clearing her throat and saying, "Not many Jamaican fathers come to see me. What can I do for you, Mr Chambers?"

"I want to know what's de answer to de chicken riddle."

Miss Watkins looked surprised.

"Oh, that," she said offhandedly. "The answer is: to get to the other side. It's an example of how pragmatists deal with unanswerable questions. They don't care what anything means, only what it does."

"Dat's de shallow answer," Alvin insisted. "Dere's a deeper answer."

"And what is that?"

"De chicken cross de road to find out if de nothing over here is also over dere."

"That's not the answer I expect. And it's my class and my riddle."

"It's my country, my road and my chicken!" Alvin countered peevishly.

"Oh, you own every chicken and every road in Jamaica? How dare you come into my classroom and tell me what my riddle means! I think you'd better leave or I'll call Security."

"Call Security?" Alvin exploded. "Dis is not a riddle. Dis is an attempt at destabilization. Dis is disinformation by the CIA ..."

"Security!" Miss Watkins shrieked.

That evening, father and daughter were on the veranda, waiting for Sylvia to come home from work. The sun had slipped behind a green mountain, and an emulsified darkness thick as cough syrup oozed over the fields of guinea grass.

"Miss Watkins said you behaved like a lunatic," Cindy scowled.

"She's just jealous because I had a better answer to her riddle. She didn't give me a chance to finish."

Alive with the clamour of insects, frogs and lizards, the land around the veranda of the great house was drenched in the undivided awfulness of night. A donkey brayed as if the unlettered beast, caught up in a moment beyond its comprehension, was bleating for help. Somewhere in the hills a dog answered by barking in the erratic tempo of a fibrillating heartbeat.

"What was your answer?"

"I was going to tell her," Alvin said cryptically, "dat it is better to pretend dat nothing is something dan to believe dat everything is nothing."

"Dat's your answer?" Cindy asked incredulously. "But what does dat mean? And what does dat have to do with why de chicken crosses de road?"

Alvin stared lovingly at his only child. He felt whole again, like a dieter who was back on red meat after losing his beloved paunch to a fiendish American vegetarian diet. Warmth and contentment oozed out of his every pore.

"You'll find out some day," he said loftily.

New Banana

MOST tourists do not like to be thought of as tourists, and James Kiwaczyk, a big-boned American of Polish descent from Chicago, was the exception only in the intensity of this feeling. He despised being thought of as a tourist. He felt that there was something ignominious about that designation, like being a professional snoop whose occupation was mindless gawking.

It was 1975, and the Kiwaczyks – James and Alice, both in their mid-twenties – were in Montego Bay on holiday. Their hotel was brand-new and loomed gleaming over a narrow strip of scruffy white-sand beach squeezed like pus out of a dark and grubby patch of limestone shoreline. With a private balcony jutting off each room, the hulking ten-storey building resembled a gaudy man-made beehive.

The ugly hotel and the skimpy beach didn't much matter to the Kiwaczyks. So long as her rump was not as fat as her mother's, Alice was happy. And James would've been happy, too, if only he didn't feel as if he was just another sheep-like tourist. Yet with the tropical sun blazing down on their heads in January while their hometown of Chicago was buried under the worst blizzard of the century, both were glad to be in Jamaica.

The Kiwaczyks, who were not rich, were in Montego Bay thanks to a horse named *Uneventful* that had run first in a race at the Arlington racetrack, paying 45 to 1 on a twenty dollar bet. Just a few hours earlier, James had been scanning the picture display window of a travel agency that featured posters of Jamaica glistening under a robust winter sun. As he stood on the sidewalk and gaped with longing at the posters, a light snow was falling. Everywhere he looked, the street and buildings were crusty with the icy white rind of winter. So as soon as he collected his winnings, he hurried back to the travel agency and impulsively bought a tour package for a week.

Three months later, the Kiwaczyks found themselves in Montego Bay.

They spent the first day browning in the relentless sun with all the other tourists. In the afternoon, the hotel's programmed entertainment, consisting of organized games and contests, only intensified James's dislike of being herded about like sheep.

"I hate being a tourist," James grumbled that night as he stepped into his pyjamas.

"Well," Alice said tartly, "you are a tourist. You're a visitor here. That makes you a tourist. I'm a tourist, too. And I don't know about you, but I'm having a good time."

They turned off the light and settled down to sleep. A few minutes later James stirred restlessly.

"There's a mosquito in here," he grumped, sitting up in bed. "He's come to drink the fresh blood of the tourists."

"Don't be ridiculous," Alice snapped. "The mosquito doesn't know we're tourists."

"Everyone knows. Everything knows. It's like we're marked."

Then he got up and turned on the light, looking for the mosquito, which drew a sharp rebuke from Alice and led to a nasty spat.

The next morning at breakfast, the Kiwaczyks were served by their new waiter, Hopeton Munro Uppinton, a Jamaican of about the same age as James.

New to waiting tables, Hopeton had been given very little training beyond being strongly advised to keep his thumbs out of the soup and water when he was serving either one. This particular morning he was careful to do that and, although a little nervous, felt quite proud of himself as he poured coffee and served a platter of bananas.

"What's wrong with these bananas?" James scowled, holding up the fruit to the light.

"What's wrong with dem, sah?" Hopeton asked, puzzled.

"They're green is what's wrong. See? Green."

"Oh no, sah. Dey're ripe, even if dey look green."

"How can a green banana be ripe?"

Hopeton was caught off guard but quickly recovered. "Because dey're new bananas, sah."

To demonstrate, he peeled one of the bananas and showed that it was indeed ripe. James looked the peeled banana up and down with distaste.

"How come I never heard of such a banana in Chicago?"

"Because it's new, sah," Hopeton put in smoothly with impeccable logic. "Taste it, sah, and you'll see dat it's ripe."

James did, found that the banana was indeed ripe and began muttering under his breath about how the public could be expected to keep up when even the very bananas were being changed right under their noses without any warning.

As he passed Hopeton at the door of the restaurant, he quipped, "Goodbye, New Banana."

"Goodbye, sah," Hopeton replied, with a diffident smile.

Another waiter whom Hopeton had caught out in the slips for a duck at the last company cricket match overheard this exchange. "Why dat man call you New Banana?" he wondered idly.

"You have to ask him dat," Hopeton muttered, heading for the kitchen.

"Hey, New Banana!" the waiter yelled derisively after Hopeton as he disappeared.

A third waiter strolled over and asked, "Who you calling New Banana?"

"Hopeton!" the second waiter chuckled with a wicked grin.

That evening, with only two days of their holiday left, the Kiwaczyks ran into the Pulaskis at the ocean-side bar. Although they knew the Pulaskis only casually in Chicago, meeting them occasionally at Little League games, being in a foreign land together made them instant best friends.

The foursome went to dinner and were waited on by Hopeton, who was working a split shift. James greeted him, "Hi, New Banana," to which Hopeton grudgingly answered, and this little intimacy, trivial as it was, visibly impressed Mr Pulaski, who remarked that clearly James was on an intimate footing with the hotel staff, more like an insider than a tourist. James was so pleased that for the rest of the night he felt encouraged to constantly chorus New Banana *this* and New Banana *that* to which Hopeton had to answer gamely or seem churlish.

Before the evening ended, the name *New Banana* had blown

into the kitchen. By the end of the dinner shift, all the crew were calling Hopeton that, no matter whom he threatened to lick down or murder outright.

For the remaining two days of his holiday, James was relentless in his use of that name, and he made a great show of New Banana-ing the poor waiter at every opportunity.

Indeed, his last words as he got into the taxi for the journey to the airport were, "Goodbye, New Banana," screamed at Hopeton, who had just got off work and was filing through the gate with other weary off-duty workers.

"Shut up!" Hopeton muttered under his breath while grinning broadly and waving cheerfully as though he was taking leave of his best friend.

The years flew past like John Crows. The Kiwaczyks began having children, and when they had a healthy one of each sex, Alice had her tubes tied, even though she was a devout Catholic. James began the slow rise to the top of his printing company and by the end of five years was in a supervisory position.

Even when they could scarcely afford it, the Kiwaczyks made a point of returning to Montego Bay at least every other year on holiday and staying at the same hotel. And James always made a point of seeking out Hopeton and hailing him familiarly in public as "New Banana". He was especially fulsome about doing it when there were other Americans around, as a way of boasting that he was not just another tourist, but really more like a regular.

Hopeton, for his part, over the years had bred four children by four different baby mothers and had to work at two jobs to help pay for their support. The name New Banana now stuck to him like a bloodsucking tick. After five years in the same position at the same hotel, he took a job as head waiter in a hotel on the outskirts of Montego Bay, where he was briefly known as Mr Uppinton.

But, as bad luck would have it, that same year the Kiwaczyks coincidentally changed to that very hotel, and James, spotting Hopeton across the dining room was so excited to see a familiar face that he bawled out, "Hey, New Banana!" drawing attention to the new head waiter's secret alias. By the end of the Kiwaczyks' stay, nearly everyone on the dining-room staff had begun to call Hopeton "New Banana".

One night during this week Hopeton felt in the mood to kill someone, he was so vexed at the turn of events. He was sitting outside his ramshackle house in Montego Bay, taking the air under a leafy ackee tree, when his thirteen-year-old son asked him why people called him "New Banana".

"Mind you own business, boy!" Hopeton snapped.

"Me just asking," the youth mumbled, slouching off.

Another flock of years flew past. Alice's rump blew up like a balloon, becoming more prodigious than her mother's at its worst. James developed a pot belly so rotund and heavy that it made him walk with a backward tilt. The Kiwaczyks' children left home and went to college, and James became part owner of the printing business where he had worked for over twenty-five years.

Hopeton became a grandfather and settled down to live with his fourth baby mother. Now in his fifties, he had acquired elder statesman's status at the hotel and was held in such high esteem that only the most senior staff dared call him New Banana. The German general manager of the hotel, for example, insisted on calling him that to the bitter end, and would have done so even if Hopeton had been lying on his deathbed. Other supervisory staff who outranked him also regularly and boastfully licked him with that hideous name, the way one might wave around a key to the executive washroom. Those below him called him New Banana only at their peril. But if he was not New Banana to his face, he was always New Banana behind his back.

On the last night of their umpteenth visit to Jamaica, the Kiwaczyks were in bed, digesting a gluttonous meal and reminiscing about their previous visits to Montego Bay. Their room was on the tenth floor and had a spectacular view of the bay and the dark surrounding mountains, sparkling with lights.

That same night, Hopeton and the baby mother with whom he had settled down were also abed, trying to discuss the day's happenings over the deafening nightly choir of barking dogs.

"New Banana looks good, doesn't he?" James remarked to Alice as they lay drowsily side by side, their full bellies swelling the bedsheets into huge twin mounds.

"Dat damn American New Banana man is in town," Hopeton was muttering to his baby mother. "I'd love to poison him."

"You must be off you head talking 'bout poisoning tourists. You want dem hang you?"

"Dat damn American man dat give me dat dutty name thirty years ago. Dem going put it on me gravestone. How would you like to have a tourist come rename you New Banana?"

"When did we first meet New Banana?"

"The time I won that money at Arlington. Must be at least thirty years ago."

"Thirty years ago! My butt was small and tight then. Now look at it."

"It's still small and tight."

"I can't tell you how I hate dat damn man for giving me dat name."

"And all dis time you never say nothing to him?"

"Say wha'? Him is a guest and me is a waiter. Wha' me fe say?"

"Liar. I've got a big butt. Just like my mother. In a bathing suit, I look like a hippopotamus."

"No, you don't."

"What do I look like, then?"

"Just say to him, 'Listen Missah Tourist, dis is Jamaica, where man love to give man nickname. Beg you, sah, stop calling me New Banana. Dat is not de name me modder did give me.'"

"You look like a dolphin."

"I've never seen a dolphin with a butt as fat as mine."

"Is not every poison dem can trace, you know. Suppose him eat unopen ackee and dead. Who dem can blame? Don't people dead from dat every year in Jamaica?"

"Hopeton, don't make dem kind o' joke 'round me, you hear?"

"Joke? Oh, you think is joke me joking?"

"You know, over the years New Banana is the one familiar face we've seen year in and year out. I kinda like the guy. He gives me a feeling of stability."

"You should tell New Banana how much you appreciate him."

"You should tell dat man how him humbug up you life."

"Goodnight, Jim."

"Goodnight."

"Boy, listen to de dog dem bark, eh, New Banana?"

"Who de backside you calling New Banana?"

"Sorry. Me never mean nuttin. It just slip out."

The next morning, bright and early, James went for a walk around the pool, catching some of the morning air that was still heavy with the night dew. Since it was his last day in Jamaica, he wanted to savour every minute. A glacial stillness lay over the empty tables and loungers arranged in rows around the pool deck. In the distance, the Caribbean gaped at the sky with a blue glass eye.

James was just about to sit down and enjoy the early morning peacefulness, when he spotted Hopeton hurrying to the kitchen.

"Hey, New Banana!" James cried, hurrying over to the waiter.

"Yes, sah," Hopeton replied sullenly, the hand in his pocket knotting into a clenched fist.

"You know, New Banana," James said, looking as embarrassed as he felt, "last night my wife and I were talking about you. I know you only see us for a week at a time, and some years you don't see us at all, but I wanted you to know how welcome and accepted you've made us feel."

They faced each other with the curious uneasiness that always crops up between men during moments of unexpected intimacy.

"Well," James said lamely, "we're leaving this afternoon for Chicago and only God knows when we will be back. I just wanted to tell you that."

Hopeton peered sharply at him.

"What time does your plane leave, sah?"

"In about five hours."

Hopeton screwed up his face in concentration as though he was working on a tricky word problem in algebra.

"You know what I'm going to do, sah?" he said carefully. "I'm going to go to the kitchen and cook you a special ackee and saltfish breakfast."

"That's wonderful! I love ackee and saltfish. And so does Alice!"

"No, dis breakfast is not for Miss Alice. Dis is for you alone. Just have a seat at one of de poolside tables, and I'll serve you meself."

"That'll be wonderful, New Banana."

"And if you don't like how it taste, you can start calling me New Ackee."

"New Ackee!" James guffawed loudly, slapping his pudgy belly at this ridiculous idea. "I don't think so! After thirty years, you'll never be anything else to me but New Banana!"

The Man Who Knew the Price of All Fish

BABA was a black man with no past. He had nothing ahead of him; he had nothing behind him. He had dropped out of oblivion one day, grew up in Montego Bay on the island of Jamaica, growing into manhood with a tremendous lower jaw burgeoning above his windpipe, a jawbone as large as the top jaw of any mastiff, a jaw that jutted out under his face disjointed, unproportioned, stiff, mysteriously heavy, capped with a lower level of green teeth. He was a black man with no past and no future, with a forehead rounded and indented like a goat's, with two thick and hirsute arms that dropped below his waist when he walked.

His eyes, which people would squint to look into, were sunk deep inside his black face, sheltered by two fat lids that dropped thick as cream, squiggled down deep into the mystery blackness of his skin, and black themselves, so that except for their shine in the sunlight, they were hidden in the camouflage of his face.

And, on top of this, he had no past. He had no future; he had no wife; he had no children; he had nothing, except a small black-hulled canoe, and some wire fishpots and mangrove-stained lines he used to catch fish with.

Every night he rowed out in his canoe and set his fishpots and threw down his lines, and every morning he rowed into Giddy Beach with a canoeful of dead fish and sold the dead fish to women as poor as himself, who would higgle him furiously, insult his fish, call him a *jinal*, meaning that he was intent on robbing them, paw over the corpses of the fish, hold him up to cynical comparison with more successful fishermen, accuse him of having a white mother, call him a Rastafarian, then walk away clutching contemptuously at the dead fish wrapped in newspaper, for which they had paid Baba's price. For it was impossible to higgle him down, because he had no past and could not be either insulted or deprecated.

It did not matter what they called his mother, because he had no mother. He had no wife they could say cuckolded him; he had no children who got poor marks at school; he had no grandfather who bubbled over his senility on street corners; he had no cousins who were cat-o'-nined for stealing; he had no aunts who painted their faces for tourist men at nights; he had no attachments which made him vulnerable to abuse; he had no one to be called into shame over.

And so no one had ever higgled him down on the price of his fish. If he said that the green-skinned, beak-teeth parrot-fish were a shilling each, it was impossible to shake him. The woman could call the fish gangrened, she could say it had a slimy skin, she could say it was not a fish, she could say anything, it would not matter. She could higgle until her black face was greener than the parrot-fish, it would not matter. For once Baba had decided that a fish was worth a shilling, God could not alter its price. The fish was always sold for a shilling.

And because he was so obdurate in his ways, and because he would not be insulted, those women who approached his canoe came to buy, not to higgle. They would gloomily pick out a fish, saying nothing about its complexion, ask him his price and dip down into their knotted handkerchiefs for the money tied up in a ball at one corner, and pay him.

Sometimes, for show, because it is obscene for a Jamaican woman to pay the asking price without a show of higgle, one or two would aim a cursory insult at the fish, ask his price once more, say "Rass clath" in contempt, kiss their teeth with disgust, fidget their fingers over the dead body of the fish with a show of reluctance, as if they knew they were to be cheated but had resigned themselves, and pay.

It was impossible to higgle Baba because he had no past. When that jaw locked with a click against the windpipe, it meant that his mind had sprung shut on the price, it meant that a terrible obduracy had fixed its mark on his face, demon stubbornness was ahold of him once again, and nothing, not piety, protestation, insult, innuendo, levity, malice, small-talk, nothing could move him.

So the only thing a woman could do, if she meant to keep her Jamaican self-respect, was to insult him or his mother. But she could not even do that because he had no past, and it did not matter. A sphinx-like solemnity would droop over his face, the cream-thick eyelids would float languidly at half-mast, that terrible jawbone would click and Baba would stand there, imperturbable, unmoved, unmovable.

It was infuriating, it was maddening to the Montego Bay women. Everyone else on the beach could be higgled, except Baba. Any other fisherman would drop his price a halfpenny if his parrot-fish were called slimy, any decent Jamaican pedlar would stir at least a farthing off his fixed price for the sake of show in the face of determined contention from a higgler, any respectable Jamaican would budge a fraction, at least to signal to God and the world a lack of obdurateness, to show others (for the sake of form) that no man can dogmatically know the universal worth of any fish. A mind that would not was holding to infallibility, was saying that of all the prices that can be made out of numbers, only one was fitted to each fish, and no other.

And that was what Baba was saying when his jaw clicked in fixity, when he attached a price to a fish and would not budge.

He did not understand the philosophy, because he did not think about it, but that was what he was saying.

There was one woman for whom he nearly shifted his price. She was new to Montego Bay and unversed in the ways of Baba. She made a frontal assault on the body of a black sam fish, claiming a graveyard stench for it. She accused Baba of selling stale bait, pointing to the green glassiness of its eyes as evidence that the fish was old. She grasped the fish by the tail and swung it lightly over the gunwales of the black-stained canoe to demonstrate from its lack of flex that it had rigor mortis. She spat tobacco out of the corner of her mouth near the tail of the fish to show contempt for its dead body and dropped it heavily into the pool of water in the bottom of the boat to show that it would not float and therefore was no longer a fish. She called down biblical imprecations on the fish and the man who would sell it for a shilling, and threw herself on the beach beside the boat, digging her fingers into the sand and swearing that she would sooner dig a grave for the fish than pay a shilling for it.

And she almost moved him.

The jaw did not immediately click, and a pyramid hardness

did not settle over his face. Instead, something miraculous appeared to happen. The black eyes peered out dubiously from under the gelatinous lids, the face sagged and the mouth almost opened.

A gasp went up among the higglers. Imprecations were broken off in mid-sentence. Silence descended on the beach as lightly as a butterfly, for it seemed, for a moment, as if Baba were about to relent, as if a melting of the biblical firmness in that jaw was about to begin; it almost seemed, no more than the hint of a seem, that Baba had been moved. He put a thick-fingered hand to the base of the jawbone, looked down dubiously at the maligned fish, and for the interminableness which tension and danger invest mere seconds with, his mind was slung between two inward peaks, settling firmly neither on one nor on the other, and he seemed like any man hanging nervously in the gap of indecision.

But it was folly to think so, for no sooner had the flurry among the canoes died down and all eyes swung over to read the symptoms of hesitancy in that massive jawbone, than the hideous click sounded, and the jawbone locked into a siege of adamantine obduracy. This time no one could move him, because he had given a second pause to his decision, and his jaw was doubly cemented in its certainty.

A cry of relief went up from the crowd of higglers. The woman who had instilled doubt renewed her hysteria with greater fever than before. She said the fish was a *rass clath* fish, a *blood clath* fish, a *bumbo clath* fish and, reaching the pinnacle of Jamaican obscenity with that last expression, she turned red with anger for using up all the superlatives available to her without relief. She moaned, rolled her eyes inside the black sockets in her face, showing their fearsome whites, and spat with contempt. She grasped the fish and attempted to mangle it. She cried that Baba was an eater of goat turd, that his fish were loathsome and diseased, that a duppy would lay hands on his mouth as he slept. She ransacked the corners and cupboards of Jamaican folklore for insults, but she could not move him. Baba was implacable. He was granite. His jawbone had clicked.

For he had no past, and he had no wife, and he had no children, and he had no property, except for the black-stained canoe and the wire fishpots and the lines he used to catch his fish. And once he had caught a fish, he fixed a price to its dead body and God himself could not dispute it.

His fish were his own. He rowed out over the deep sea at night with a kerosene lamp in the bow of his canoe, and all night he dropped lines and traps to the bottom, floating on the blackness of the deep with only the skin of the cotton-tree canoe between him and its terrors. All night he stayed there, pulling up the struggling fish from the bottom of the black sea, which licked the sides of his canoe peacefully, heaved him up and down, rolled him on the dreamy somnolence of a night swell, and when he held a fish between his fingers, took the hook out of its gasping jaws, strangled it between his heavy forefinger and thumb, or smashed its head against the bottom of the canoe, it became his, and for the rest of the night he rode in the bottom of the boat with the bodies of the fish and had time to discover the true price of each.

The green parrot-fish, the yellowtail snapper, the thick black sam, the red congo tony, they all died in the bottom of the boat sucking dry at the night wind, their gills beating furiously, their eyes stiffening into the glassiness of death, and under the blue starlight Jamaican night an enormous jawbone sat over them brooding.

For they were his own, he had dropped his lines into the dreaming sea, and he had pulled them up one by one out of its blackness. When he rowed into Giddy Beach in the morning, the sun would be rising over the Bogue Islands on his left, and the body of every dead fish would have its rightful price.

The Trip to Paris

ANCEL Pendergast tapped his foot impatiently on the polished hardwood floor, making the sound of a courting beetle, and cast a critical eye over Monica, his wife of forty years, who was planted in front of the vanity unit, peering at her reflection in the mirror and caulking every unsightly pore on her dark-brown face with deft strokes of a liquid foundation. They were soon to be on their way to Paris (as in Paris, France) yet she was being so slow and poky-poky that one would think that they were just popping next door to see a neighbour.

"It's not every day we get to go to Paris, you know, Monica," he muttered. "We don't want to be late!"

She would soon be finished, she murmured, deep in concentration, cocking her head to one side like a peering bird so she could better view her profile.

"I just don't want to miss de plane," he said lamely.

She replied that in more than forty years of marriage she'd never caused them to miss a bus much less a plane, and she wasn't about to start now.

Outside the brightly-lit bedroom the rooms of their enormous house gaped dark and cavernous, its expensive furnishings standing stiffly at attention in the dimness.

When Monica was finally ready, she stood up and announced that she had done all that she could to beat back the ravages of nature. This was the best she could look at sixty-five.

She was now prepared to face the fault-finding French.

The Pendergasts were old-fashioned Jamaicans who, over the years, had grown rich. Their house was in a tony district of DeKalb County (with the *l* never pronounced by those who knew better) where the homeowners were mostly black and faithfully drove only expensive German cars whose second name began with *B*.

Both Pendergasts were originally from Malvern in the hills of Jamaica, sharing a common braising in a stewpot of discipline, ambition and love of everything foreign. In grammar school, they had chanted rhymes about the vital statistics of European rivers and mountains and memorized the names of dead European despots, some of whose effigies still straddled bronze horses in public parks.

Given this upbringing, it was inevitable that they would eventually take flight, like spores, and be blown away to foreign soil. This they had done nearly forty years ago, eventually settling in Atlanta, Georgia, where they raised a family that had since scattered throughout the American continent. Now the Pendergasts were at an age where they felt they had been left dangling on the family tree, like the useless husks of opened pods.

Along the way Ancel had grown rich in the time-honoured American way – by selling the best years of his life to Mammon. It was hardly unexpected. Raised in the Malvernian motto "Always striving, always seeking", he had been propelled by this platitude over the years from being a carpenter to a builder to a developer, making him richer and richer with every leap .

And with the money and the array of choices came Monica's urgent and exotic craving for Paris.

Where this appetite had come from neither of them knew, but Ancel suspected its origin was Mrs Kendrick's geography class in 1948, which was stuffed with facts and details about France. It was the only foreign land Mrs Kendrick had ever visited in her life (she was now dead, God rest her soul), sent there to learn French pedagogical methods while she was at the Ministry of Education. She had spent a year in Paris sopping up the French system before being re-posted to Malvern as a geography teacher. From then on, every geography lesson Mrs Kendrick taught, no matter if its main focus was the river Nile or the Argentine Pampas, somehow included references to France.

Monica first proposed in 1996 that they go to Paris to celebrate their fortieth wedding anniversary, and although Ancel was then heavily involved in tight negotiations over a real-estate assemblage deal, just to please her, he unthinkingly agreed. They made the airline reservations, hotel bookings and planned an itinerary. But at the last minute Ancel simply couldn't tear himself away from business. Monica was visibly disappointed. A few days later she cheered up when Ancel bought her an expensive new car with a hyphenated name.

Monica tried again for Paris two years later, and again they made the arrangements. But this time, on the very eve of their departure, a new mega-deal popped up that required Ancel's unique touch and forced another cancellation.

On the evening that they were to have left, Ancel arrived home late to find Monica weeping her heart out in the bedroom. He rushed to her side, concern brimming in his tired eyes.

"We'll never get to Paris!" Monica wailed.

Ancel hugged her protectively. "Of course we will."

"I just wanted us to be together in Mrs Kendrick's land," Monica sobbed, shaking as if she'd been struck by a malarial chill.

"Mrs Kendrick was from Trelawny," Ancel said carefully. "But one day we'll go. I swear on Mummy's grave!"

Monica was appeased. If it was one thing Malvernians were known for, it was love of Mummy. No oath could be more solemn, sacred and unbreakable than one that threatened Mummy's eternal rest.

She believed her husband and gave him an adoring hug and kiss, for now she knew. They were definitely going to Paris.

So now in 2001, the trip was finally on.

It began with some anomalies, such as the limo driver's observation that whereas Ancel's suitcase was as heavy as lead, Monica's was as light as a feather. Ancel pointed out that a man's clothing was heavier than a woman's and said so in such a sharp tone that the white driver shut up and was sullen the rest of the way to the airport.

Then the stupid Delta stewardess tried to put someone else in Monica's seat, causing Ancel to raise a stink about how he'd bought and paid for two first-class tickets, yet a woman couldn't even go to the bathroom aboard a stinking Delta jet without having her seat sold out from under her.

During the eight and a half hour flight Monica did not even eat a scrap of food. She was just too afraid of putting on weight, and at her age every pound added would be nearly impossible to take off.

So she ate nothing. Ten hours later, Ancel found himself in a swanky five-star hotel room in downtown Paris.

"Well," he said triumphantly to Monica, "we're here." And he stared at his reflection in a French wall mirror.

Staring back at him with Malvernian steeliness was a short black man in his sixties with thinning grey hair and a soft belly, as rounded and globular as a beach ball. He was finally in Paris, but he looked the same as he did in Atlanta.

They did all the Parisian things that Monica had always wanted to do, Ancel following his wife around like a house-broken puppy. They ate lunch in a sidewalk café near the Place de la Paix, strolled the Champs-Elysées at night, ogled the Eiffel Tower, and took a dinner cruise on the Seine.

At first, the staff of the five-star hotel was standoffish and coolly polite to them, as if they were *nouveau riche*, but Ancel began tipping generously and soon everywhere they showed their faces on the premises, they were showered with effusive *bonjours* or *bonsoirs*, as if they were celebrities.

They explored massive cathedrals, La Madeleine and the Sacré Coeur, and were reduced to a shocked gawking at the overwhelming ornateness and grandeur draining down on their humbly bowed heads from a thousand overhead nooks and crannies and ledges. Statues, intricate friezes, massive paintings, stained-glass images, cryptic heraldic symbols, it was all too much for Malvernian eyes used to simplicity and starkness, and both Monica and Ancel felt as dazzled as if they had been peering too hard at the noonday Jamaican sun.

They hurried from the Sacré Coeur and out into the *rue*, where Monica remarked that the French God certainly had a taste for sumptuousness. Ancel said as far as he knew God was the same God all over the world, but Monica demurred and replied that her God was Jesus and she was quite sure that Jesus preferred a hut to a palace and would not approve of this wastefully expensive cathedral. Ancel had no good answer because, not being a churchgoer himself, he felt theologically unqualified to pass judgment on the Almighty's working budget.

After a week and a half of Paris, they were ready to go home, and on their last night in the "City of Lights", they lay quietly nestled in each other's arms like the old lovers they were and Monica whispered, "Thank you, my husband, for carrying me to Paris," to which Ancel answered drowsily just before he fell asleep, "You're welcome, my darling."

It had cost him $15,000 but it had been worth every penny to keep his life's mate happy. On this comforting thought, Ancel fell asleep entwined in the arms of his beloved.

Malvernians do not flinch at jet lag, and the day after returning to Atlanta found Ancel buried in business up to his nose-bridge. He put in a full day answering umpteen phone calls and writing a ton of letters and e-mails, keeping Hilda, his long-time secretary, feverishly occupied.

He returned home late that night, wearily trudging into the kitchen as the automatic garage door opener hummed quietly behind him and the security system allowed him entry with electronic unctuousness. The telephone answering machine was splattering the walls of the darkened kitchen with arterial blood, telling him he had a message on his private line whose number was known to only a few people with whom his life was deeply entwined.

He pushed the *play* button and heard the voice of his youngest child, a graduate of Harvard and now a senior vice president for an investment firm in Philadelphia.

"Dad, it's Rachel," she said crisply in the shrill tone of one still young enough to think that the world can be reformed by a scolding. "I can't believe you went to Paris with Mummy dead less than a month. You know she always wanted to go there with you. Well, you've been and you can't un-go, although I can't imagine what you had in mind. Call me as soon as you get home. We need to talk!"

With the last sentence still lingering in the room like the smell of yesterday's roses, the machine clicked twice and reset itself, and an ancient loneliness settled around the empty house like a closing mouth.

Ancel stirred, making his chair squeak, and turned to look for his wife, who would ordinarily be found in the den, embroidering.

His footfalls sounded a sorrowful weariness as he waded into the empty room through a silence as thick and cloying as jelly, looking like a mourner slow-marching to a dirge.

"It was Rachel," he said softly to a vacant easy chair. "She thinks I went to Paris without you."

They both exploded in hearty laughter.

The Thief

HEMLYN Owen cultivated forty acres of land in the district of Endeavor, near Stewart Town, where he had lived for over thirty years, raising pigs and goats. A religious man who was an elder in the Pentecostal church, Hemlyn and his wife, Hyacinth, shared a modest cottage in the cool shadows of the Dry Harbour Mountains. There they had raised one son, who worked as an electrician for a large North Coast hotel.

One year, quite by accident, Hemlyn discovered a tomato vine growing at the side of his house. He had not planted it, but perhaps he or Hyacinth had happened to spit a tomato seed out of the window and it had fallen on fertile soil. However the plant had happened, he got from it a bountiful yield of some ten tomatoes.

This discovery encouraged him to try his hand at planting tomatoes, and with his only workman, Joseph, at his side he dug holes in a garden bed and put in a dozen tomato seeds. Much to his amazement, nearly all the seeds took and the plants bore fruit. Before long he had a whole garden devoted to tomatoes. People in the district found out and began to come and buy tomatoes from him. One weekend alone, he and Hyacinth collected over a thousand US dollars selling tomatoes.

Hemlyn consulted the agricultural officer in the district, and with the man's advice he planted half an acre in tomatoes. The district had only recently been electrified, and Hemlyn could not afford any irrigation, but his fields were blessed with a gentle rain nearly every afternoon, and soon vegetable vendors were driving their battered pick-up trucks to his front yard to buy tomatoes for resale across the island. One particularly good weekend, the Owens sold ten thousand US dollars in tomatoes.

Hemlyn used the money to invest in fertilizer and began to plan an expansion of his tomato fields. His son came to visit, and there was talk of selling the tomatoes directly to the hotel for which the son worked, fresh tomatoes being a favourite among tourists and hard to find on the island.

One morning Hemlyn woke up to find that a thief had struck his tomato fields. In one corner it was as if locusts had stripped the plants bare. The vines sagged from being manhandled during the night, and not a single ripe tomato was left on them.

Like most cultivators, Hemlyn had a bottomless hatred for thieves who committed praedial larceny. Joseph, his workman, felt exactly the same way, and as they strolled through the stripped corner of the field, there was much bitter muttering between them about what they would do if they could catch the person responsible. Hyacinth, when she was told about their misfortune, spoke in exactly the same hot-blooded vein. No death, disease or suffering would be vile or painful enough punishment for the tomato thief to suit her.

Hemlyn went to the police and reported the theft, and the district constable rode over on his Quickly moped and took a formal report. He walked the fields with Hemlyn, expressing sympathy over his loss, which the constable also felt keenly, being himself a struggling grower.

"A thief like dat should be killed," Hemlyn scowled.

"Killed?" the constable sputtered. "Killed without suffering is too quick for a thief. Anybody who would thief somebody else's crop is not a man. Him is a dog."

"I wish I could catch him in de act", Joseph muttered darkly, "so I could chop him up."

"Chop him up?" the constable snorted derisively. "Chopping is too good for one like him."

All these sentiments, and even more bloodthirsty ones, were heartily seconded by Hyacinth that evening as the constable filled out his formal report over a rum.

That weekend, Hemlyn went to the market in Stewart Town and suspiciously eyed every higgler selling tomatoes. He went so far as to question one old woman about where she had purchased her tomatoes, and when she told him she had bought from a wholesaler in Brown's Town, he acted as though he didn't believe her. He was in a bitter and vengeful mood that day as he strolled morosely among the higglers, sitting with their wares spread out on the dirty concrete floor of the market, and he exchanged only curt remarks with the few people who recognized him.

For the next week he slept badly, and several times he started up out of bed, padded to the window of his cottage and peered out into the night, thinking he had heard the thief. One night, he spotted a shadow slinking among the trees and, getting his shotgun from his closet, he stalked out into the darkness, hoping to catch the thief red-handed. But the slinking shadow turned out to be one of his goats, and he returned to his bed disappointed.

Things settled down eventually, and Hemlyn resumed his tomato farming.

About one month later, the thief struck again, this time wiping out nearly a quarter of the tomato crop in one section of a field.

Hemlyn, Joseph and Hyacinth were beside themselves with rage. Reporting the theft again to the police seemed pointless. What was required, they decided in the conference held late one night on the veranda of the small cottage, was an ambush. Hemlyn and Joseph would wait for the crop to begin bearing again, then they would spend a night or two in the fields, hoping the thief would return and they could catch him in the act.

Over the next few weeks Hemlyn and Joseph continued to work hard on cultivating the tomatoes. They began to regard the vegetables not as a crop, but as bait, and as they worked on their hands and knees, they often spoke in bloody terms about what they would do to the thief when they caught him. They called him a dog, a John Crow, a nasty brute, a worthless wretch and many other names. This chorused vilification brought them closer together, and made the time spent in the hot fields fly past quickly. At nights, as Hemlyn and Hyacinth sat on the front porch of their small cottage, husband and wife would take turns cursing the thief and calling down God and the Devil on the unknown criminal.

One night, Hemlyn decided that the trap was baited and ready, that if ever the thief were to strike again, it would be tonight.

He loaded up both barrels of his shotgun with cartridges normally used to shoot baldpate on the wing. He dressed in warm clothes and set out with Joseph to spend the night lurking in ambush in the fields. Hyacinth made them a thermos of sweetened hot tea and stood on the front porch calling out encouragement as she watched them tramp off in the thickening darkness.

Hemlyn had the surge of excitement he normally felt when setting out on a bird shoot. Joseph, who had often spotted for him during the bird season, felt exactly the same tingling thrill. The two men carried blankets with them so they could snatch a few winks of sleep on the hard ground as they waited to ambush the thief.

It was the night of a full moon, and a soft breeze off the mountain slopes stirred the air. From the cool glow of the moon, they were able to make out copses of trees, the gentle pleats and folds of the land, the Dry Harbour Mountains looming dark, bony and ominous behind them and the rows and rows of neatly staked tomato plants arranged in prissy formation, as if they were on display at an agricultural fair.

They settled down in the shadow of an East Indian mango tree and waited.

The two ambushers spoke in whispers, but really had little of meat to say to each other since one was the master and the other a hired garden boy. The full moon sailed over the sharp, dark rim of the mountains, partially dissolving the clumpy shadows in a soft saffron glow.

Hemlyn began drifting in and out of sleep, for he had always been a good sleeper with a clear conscience who dropped off quickly as soon as his head hit the pillow. Several times during the night, Joseph had to shake him to wake him up, reminding his employer respectfully that he had to stay awake since he was the only one armed. Eventually, after some whispered squabbling, they decided to take turns and watch in one-hour shifts.

When it was his turn to watch, Hemlyn had to fight very hard to stay awake. He had to avoid staring too intently at the dancing fireflies, for their erratic bobbing and weavings made him drowsy.

Around three o'clock in the morning, as Joseph was on watch, he spotted a flitting shadow skulking towards the tomato plants. Joseph shook Hemlyn and pointed a trembling finger at the slinking figure.

Hemlyn, his heart racing, hoisted the gun to his shoulder and carefully cocked the left barrel, making the tiniest click. He levelled the barrel at the approaching figure, which darted from tree to tree, slinking from one patch of shadows to another without a rustle. Hemlyn tracked the figure in the gunsight as it drew stealthily closer. Joseph gripped his employer by the shoulder and squeezed him hard and familiarly in the excitement.

The thief vanished in the shadow of a tree only to reappear a few heartbeats later to scurry across one of the dark fields, into the crop. Hemlyn, the moving shadow pinned on the bead of the gunsight, could hardly breathe, he was so tense. When the garden boy started to whisper something to him, Hemlyn cut him short with an abrupt gesture.

The thief was closer now, in the middle of the tomato rows, and busily picking the vegetables, loading them up in a crocus bag. He was working at a feverish pace, occasionally stopping to glance nervously around.

"Halt!" Hemlyn cried, suddenly stepping out of the shadow of the tree.

The man dropped the bag with a gasp of surprise and whirled to face the challenge, just as Hemlyn pulled the trigger.

The gun spat a blinding tongue of fire with a roar that whiplashed off the flanks of the Dry Harbour Mountains in a deafening thunderclap. The figure was blasted off its feet and hurled violently to the ground.

"You get him!" Joseph cried. "You get him!"

They lit a kerosene lantern and carefully approached the thief, who was writhing on the ground, making a loud bubbling, which sounded like a burst standpipe. In the flickering light, they could see that the blast of the shotgun had blown a pulpy red crater over his heart through which thick clumps of blood bubbled.

"Rass!" Joseph murmured. "Me know him!"

"Me dead," the thief gasped, sputtering his words through a mouthful of bloody clots. "Joseph, is you shoot me?"

"No, is Missah Owen. Since when you turn thief, Uriah?"

"Is de first time," the dying man gasped.

"How you mean, is de first time?" Hemlyn snapped. "Is not you thief me all dis time?"

"No, sah! Lawd Jesus, me can't breathe!"

The blood was oozing from the chest wound in thick muddy gobs. The thief put his hand to the pulpy wound, pulling back his fingers with a cringe of horror.

Just then, they heard the sound of footsteps running and saw a flashlight jerkily slashing the darkness.

"Don't shoot!" Hyacinth shrieked as she ran towards them. "Is me! Is Hyacinth!"

Soon she was standing beside Hemlyn and staring down at the mortally wounded thief, who made a guttural sound like that of a rutting animal.

"Him bleeding heavy," Hyacinth whispered. "Hemlyn, what we going to do now?"

"What can we do? Dere's no doctor within miles of here. Dere's no hospital. By de time we get a doctor, him bound to dead. Plus, dey always say you not supposed to remove evidence."

"So, you going leave him out here to dead?"

"What else can I do?"

"Maybe we can stop de bleeding," Hyacinth panted, sounding as if she, too, were having trouble breathing. "Maybe we can get some towels and pack de wound. What you think, Hemlyn?"

"If you never thief from me, me wouldn't shoot you," Hemlyn scolded the thief, his voice unnaturally shrill.

"I going get some towels," Hyacinth said, racing off into the darkness towards the house.

She returned a few minutes later, bent over the thief and jammed the towels into the gaping opening in his chest. Within seconds, the thick cloth was soppy and gooey with blood. The wounded thief moaned.

"Hemlyn, what we going to do?" Hyacinth asked breathlessly.

Hemlyn did not know what to do and he said so. He thought they should wait until the man died and then send Joseph to Stewart Town for the constable to bring the police van for the body. He whispered all this in an aside to Hyacinth while Joseph slumped wearily under the East Indian mango tree. The thief gave another groan and tried to roll himself over on his side, where he lay curled up and still.

"Maybe him dead," Hyacinth said hopefully.

Hemlyn bent down and put his finger against the man's throat and felt blood still faintly pulsing through the thick veins that lined the side of his neck.

"No," he said. "Him heart still pumping."

They huddled under the tree in a small, frightened circle and waited.

The country night had fully recovered from the shattering blast of the shotgun and was once again fluttering with the peaceful sounds of croaking lizards and whistling frogs. The full moon, bloated and puffy with a waterish light, sank slowly towards the skyline.

Finally, Joseph broke the silence. "You know," he mumbled darkly, "me believe is long division make Uriah turn thief."

"Stop chatting rubbish!" Hemlyn snapped edgily.

"Is true, sah! Me and him go school together. And one time de teacher give us a long division problem, but Uriah couldn't do it. No matter how de teacher beat him and beat him and beat him – and teacher beat him at least six time dat day – Uriah just couldn't understand long division. Den him stop coming to school. When me see him and ask him what happen, him say long division too hard for him and him can't manage it. Is long division make him turn thief, sah."

A breeze began to blow off the mountain slopes, rattling the leaves of the darkened trees and shrubs, making the clattering sound of small, loose bones.

"I can't believe we're just sitting here while dat poor man dies in our field," Hyacinth muttered in a small voice.

"Is not my fault," Hemlyn grumbled. "I was only protecting our crop."

"Is de teacher fault, sah," Joseph said shrilly. "Some brains just not big enough to understand long division."

The dying man began a hideous gurgling which sounded like no sound that could ever come from a man's throat. Hyacinth shuddered and stood up.

"I can't bear to listen to dis any more," she said. "I'm going in de house."

Hemlyn jumped up. "I'm coming, too."

Joseph scrambled to his feet. "Me not staying out here by meself!" he squealed.

"We can't just leave de poor man out here to die alone!" Hyacinth protested.

"Joseph," Hemlyn ordered, "you stay out here with him."

"But is not me shoot him, Missah Owen! Is you!" Joseph bawled.

They were milling around in the shadow of the East Indian mango tree, wondering what to do, when the loud animal gurgling coming from the dying man suddenly stopped, and only the sounds of croaking lizards and whistling frogs could be heard on the night breeze.

Hyacinth suggested that maybe the man had died and told Joseph to check him with a touch.

"Me not touching no deader, ma'am!" Joseph shuddered with revulsion.

Suddenly, from the crumpled body erupted a loud moan followed by childlike howls of "Grandmumma! Grandmumma! Grandmumma!"

"Lawd Jesus, what is dis now?" Hyacinth groaned, caulking her ears with her fingers.

"Him live with him grandmumma on the road beside de bridge," Joseph whispered.

"Grandmumma!" the man bleated, jerking convulsively in the muddy pool of blood in which his torn body was mired.

"Me God, Hemlyn," Hyacinth cried, "why couldn't you have just killed him and gotten it done with?"

Hemlyn thrust the gun angrily at her. "Here's de gun! Do better if you think you can!"

The man fell silent and only the usual sounds of a Jamaican country night could be heard.

"I think him dead at last," Joseph whispered.

Hemlyn bent down and touched the body that lay twisted at an unnatural angle on the darkly soiled ground.

He stood up slowly and nodded. Dawn was breaking over the ridge of the mountains and a runny light was seeping across the tomato fields.

In silence, they slogged wearily towards the small cottage gradually solidifying in the early morning dimness.

"I just wish I didn't know de name of dat thief," Hyacinth muttered.

"Uriah Bailey, ma'am!" Joseph said eagerly, proud of being able to lord knowledge over his employers. "Uriah used to live with him grandmumma near where de road run 'cross de bridge, and him couldn't do long division no matter how hard teacher beat him."

Hemlyn stared at Joseph, then without warning he stopped in his tracks, abruptly crumpled to his knees and burst into a loud, ghastly wailing.

Dawn Song

SHE was going home to attend the wedding of her god-daughter, but as she stood in front of a full-length mirror in her bedroom and slowly rotated to scan her reflection, she came to a shocking conclusion: her bottom had grown fat. It tagged along behind her, big and monstrous, like a half-opened parachute. In Kingston, her friends would notice and suss-suss in tittering huddles about how poor Maud had gone to America to live and returned home with a fat bottom for her trouble.

Never mind that she had made a good life for herself in America, even if she said so herself. She owned a small but thriving flower shop in the lobby of a posh hotel where she had two employees and did a brisk business. Last year she grossed $325,000 and paid herself a salary of $65,000. Her car was nearly new. The mortgage on her home, a tidy cottage near Stone Mountain Park, was paid off.

But her childhood friends and companions would see none of these sterling accomplishments. It had been five years since she had been home, and she would appear to them as nothing more than the dreadful spectacle of a fat bottom.

Maybe, she told herself hopefully, it wasn't that bad. What she needed was another point of view, and she glanced around the empty bedroom as if she expected miraculously to find there someone who could give her a second opinion. But she lived alone, and with no one else in the room, she asked her reflection, "Tell me de truth: is my bottom fat?"

"Yes," her reflection replied bluntly.

Such appalling frankness made her sigh aloud and quiver from head to toe as she stared grimly at herself. She saw a stout, matronly brown woman peering back at her with the expressionless face of a trusting milch cow.

Thirty-five years ago she had left Jamaica in her twenties, a pretty young woman with firm flesh, a spotless brown complexion and a figure blessed with beguiling curves. Now that she was in her late fifties, she was returning home as a dowdy matron with a wrinkled face and a bottom that was as huge and protruding as the single hump of a dromedary.

It was no use. Nothing could be done. She would wear the tightest girdle she owned and pray that no one would notice her fat bottom.

In this despairing mood she packed, occasionally pausing to scan her reflection, and when each glance confirmed the awful truth, she sighed again and again, making the melancholy peeps of a fledgling ousted from its nest.

She arrived in Jamaica the following day around mid-afternoon and clambered down the aircraft ramp into the moist, unrinsed mouth of Kingston. Reeling with the weariness and disorientation that comes from flying, she crossed the tarmac, followed the pedestrian tunnel and found herself standing like a penitent before a uniformed immigration officer.

The sullen official, properly bored and studiously indifferent, like the good civil servant he was, barely glanced at her.

So she was stunned to hear him gruffly ask, "How come you bottom so fat?" as he stamped her passport.

"What did you say?" she asked incredulously.

"Long time you don't come back," the man said impassively. "What you think me say?" he asked, pricking her with a sharp stare.

She mumbled, "Never mind!" and hurried away to get her luggage.

Outside, among the sidewalk throng of vendors, hangers-on, touts and greeters, she found them waiting for her – Marjorie, her best friend for as long as she could remember, and Marjorie's only child, Alice, whose wedding she had come to Jamaica to attend. After a joyful exchange of hugs and kisses, the three women bundled friskily into a car and sped off exuberantly through the crowded parking lot.

Her first night was a restless one. The three of them had gone nightclub-hopping and hadn't returned to the stylish upper St Andrew home until well past midnight. Settled in the guest room in a strange bed, Maud couldn't fall asleep.

The barking of dogs, the constant serenade of a Kingston night, exploded all over the darkness like small-arms fire. A croaking lizard inside the room began an arrhythmic grunting that sounded as if the beast were inches from her earhole, and several times she got up, turned on the light and combed the garishly lit room for the creature, with no luck. As soon as she switched off the light and the room was flooded with a tidal wave of darkness, the grunting noise would erupt again, like an urchin's taunt.

Early the next morning she shambled into the kitchen, hoping for a cup of tea. The maid, a wiry woman named Hilda, looking as rumpled and dishevelled as if she, too, had just got out of bed, greeted her by muttering, "Why dis fat-bottom woman up so early, eh?"

"I beg your pardon," Maud said savagely. "What did you say about me?"

"Say 'bout you, ma'am? Me no say nothing 'bout you."

"If my bottom is fat, it's none of your business!"

The maid began a rapid-fire blinking.

"Lawd Jesus! Me no say one word 'bout you bottom, mum. Me is a Christian. We not talk 'bout dem something."

"I know what I heard! I'm not deaf."

Still in her housecoat, Marjorie heard the fuss and hurried into the kitchen, yawning.

"What happen?"

"She said my bottom was fat!"

"What? Hilda's a Seventh Day Adventist!"

"Miss Marjorie, Jesus bear me witness. Me no say nothing to de woman! Me poor, poor sinner! Me only say, 'Good morning, you want coffee or tea for breakfast?'"

Hung-over and bedraggled from the previous night's spree, an obviously weary Alice staggered into the kitchen.

"It's my wedding day," she complained in a sulky voice. "What's de row all about?"

"My bottom is not fat!" Maud declared stridently.

"Who said it was?"

"Your domestic helper."

"Me never say nothing, Miss Alice!" Hilda yowled indignantly.

"Is dis all dere is to life?" Alice sighed.

"My bottom is not dat fat," Maud sputtered, "and if it is, it's because life in America is not easy. You should try it yourself sometime and see how it changes you."

"We might just do dat," Alice said, grazing her mother with a glance. "Roger wants to move to California next year."

Marjorie exploded. "What? I never heard dis before! What about me? What'll I do all by myself?"

With a touch of self-righteousness, Maud said, "You soon find out dat life abroad is not easy. Is dog eat dog."

"We're young," Alice shrugged. "If we have to eat dog, we'll eat dog."

"I'll be all alone in Jamaica!"

" I'm all alone in Atlanta."

"Me know dat me conscience is clear," Hilda rumbled from the next room. "Me never say nothing 'bout nobody bottom, for me heart belong to Jesus." Then she flounced back into the kitchen and she began raucously spewing out the hymn "What a friend we have in Jesus" in a quavering voice, as shaky and atonal as the quack of a duck.

The three women at the table shuddered.

"Good maids are hard to find dese days," Marjorie whispered conspiratorially to Maud. "At least Hilda sings hymns when she's mad. My friend's neighbour's gets drunk."

"You have to count your blessings," Maud said sarcastically.

"My dear," Marjorie nodded, patting her friend's hand as if they shared a secret.

The three women, after a frenzy of preparation and endless fussing over details, drove that afternoon to the church. There were problems with the bridal veil, the train looked soiled and unkempt, and the inevitable attack of nerves zinged through the household like an electric shock. But eventually, everything settled down and they were on their way to the Half-Way-Tree church and the wedding.

It was a nostalgic ride for Marjorie, now widowed, as she had been married to Alice's father in the same church forty years earlier.

On the way, they half-listened to the parliamentary debates being broadcast live on the radio. As usual the opposition members were asking rude questions of the prime minister during the give-and-take, and the talk waffled back and forth tediously over various stultifying topics. In the front seat sat the bride, as white and fluffy as a swollen marshmallow.

The car was edging its way through traffic when some parliamentarian backbencher suddenly asked for clarification on the present government's policy on allowing the return of fat-bottomed Jamaicans.

"My heavens! Don't these people have anything better to do wid their time dan talk about returning fat-bottom Jamaicans?"

A sickly silence greeted this outburst. Marjorie shot her friend a look of sympathy and concern in the rear-view mirror.

Stuffed in her starchy white dress, Alice turned and glared at her godmother. "Auntie Maud," she said testily, "please don't go mad and mash up me wedding."

Marjorie turned off the radio. The car inched to a stop as bumper-to-bumper traffic began crawling with the lurching, lumbering motion of a multi-jointed centipede.

"Tomorrow," Marjorie said, "we'll go to Dr Silveria and discuss what you've been hearing. He'll give you a pill."

"Do doctors have a pill for a delusion about a fat bottom?" the bride asked cynically.

Nobody had an answer, so a grim silence overtook the car as all three women stared raptly out of the window at the streets overflowing with jostling pedestrians and the battered cars, old buses and belching trucks that streamed off Hope Road and into the intersection of Half-Way-Tree in a landslide of screeching, clattering vehicles.

"I wonder if he'll be too big for me," the bride mumbled.

"What?" Marjorie blurted out, slamming on the brakes to avoid a pushcart.

"We've never done anything. I've never even seen him naked."

"It'll hurt the first time," Maud said firmly, "but after dat, you'll enjoy it."

"Don't tell her dat!" Marjorie bawled. "You'll ruin her sex life."

"Oh, for God's sake! Did it hurt you de first time, Auntie Maud?"

"Yes, it did."

"So what'd you do?"

"I just lay dere and took it. And after dat I began to enjoy myself."

They pulled into the parking lot of the church where cars were piled together in an ungeometrical hodgepodge typical of

Kingstonians. Standing with his party at the door was the groom, who, spotting the bridal car, lit up with a palpable radiance.

"He's glad to see me," Alice murmured happily.

"Of course he's glad to see you!" Marjorie snapped. "He's marrying you."

"Still," Maud muttered, "it's nice to be welcomed."

Moving gingerly in her bridal cocoon, Alice stepped clumsily out of the car and began a lurching walk towards the church door where the groom stood stock-still and beaming in his tuxedo, eyeing his bride like a hungry brown penguin.

The second night, with the excitement all over and her goddaughter legally consigned to the arms of one Joseph Williams, an accountant with ambition, Maud slept a little better. The wedding celebration had passed without a hitch and although Maud thought she overheard a few women whispering evil comments about her bottom, she made a stern effort to treat all her old acquaintances sweetly and ignore their critical, measuring looks.

The next morning she sat on the veranda feeling as if her soul was divided into two dark continents: the young woman who had been raised in one land, and the full-grown adult who had spent most of her years in another. Now that she was back in the land of her birth and youth, the memories blossomed within her like wild flowers after a broken drought. She began to remember parties she had attended many ages ago, boys she had dated, and young men she had briefly loved.

Marjorie joined her on the veranda, sipping a cup of tea.

"You ever wonder where the years went?" Maud asked, peering hard at her childhood friend with a look of longing.

Marjorie ignored the question and spoke bluntly the speech she had spent the last hour rehearsing as she lay in bed. "Maud, you think everyone is talking about your fat bottom. Dat's not normal. You need to see my doctor."

"Excuse me. My bottom is not fat!"

"It's fatter than it used to be."

"So's yours."

"Maybe so. But I don't think that everyone is talking about it."

A lingering silence fell over the veranda.

All around her the breeze, the distant hills, the earth, the sky were laden with a richness of familiar sights, sounds and smells that made Maud tingle with the joy of homecoming. Beyond the edge of the veranda oozed a scrubby front lawn fringed with the kind of trees and bushes she had first seen through the sectioning bars of the crib. Kingston at dawn smelled just as she remembered it, like a freshly lit coal stove. And this morning she had heard the land singing as it awoke from its dreamless sleep.

The familiar song, wafted on a soft morning breeze, was the same one hummed every dawn by a spontaneous choir of roosters, insects and birds, whose mingled cries drifted over the Liguanea Plains in a soprano, an *a cappella* chorus of joy.

Her father used to say that every morning the land sang a joyful welcome to the dawn, cleansing it of darkness. Many mornings in her youth Maud had lain abed and listened to this strange, comforting chorus at daybreak, sharing her delight in the dawn song with her mother and father. Now both of them were gone, leaving her stranded with a handful of childhood friends.

Maud began to sob. She could not help herself. Marjorie hurried to her side, caught the mood and also burst into tears.

"Maud," Marjorie said in a small voice, "my husband is dead. My only child is married. I'm going to be all alone."

"Like me," Maud gasped between sniffles.

"I want my husband back. I want my daughter back."

"I want my old bottom back."

"Your bottom was always fat."

"You trying to provoke me? Don't you see I'm already crying?"

"Jesus is the answer!" Hilda hawked boldly from the drawing room, where she had been eavesdropping in a remnant of darkness.

"Mind your own business!" Marjorie barked.

"Stop saying that my bottom is fat!" Maud sobbed.

Without mercy, Hilda began bellowing in the kitchen, "What a friend we have in Jesus", while on the veranda, the two friends sobbed openly in each other's arms.

Overhead in the dawn sky a solitary John Crow wheeled, unwinding like the coiled spring of an old grandfather clock.

The New Headmaster

THE new headmaster of Cornwall College was a brown man who had an ink-drawn line where other men have a mouth. He had no lips and, since he never smiled, no one could tell if he had any teeth. He was a man whose face might as well have been made of stone, for it was always blank and expressionless like a pebble.

Every morning he appeared on the veranda in front of four hundred boys lined up alphabetically by form and class. His stare, sharp and bitter like a scorpion sting, would prick at the throng, bringing a glacial silence and an unnatural stillness to the assembly. Then the classes would file into the dining room to sing hymns and be treated to the reading of a Bible lesson.

The headmaster was very vain about earning his BA from Oxford, and to be sure that the world did not forget this accomplishment, he always put *(Oxon.)*, the abbreviated Latinate term for Oxford, on his letterhead and calling card. He couldn't quite manage an Oxford accent because of his Jamaican upbringing, but he tried his best to sound, if not as stuffy as an Oxford don, at least as cryptic.

He and his family, which consisted of a wife and two daughters, settled into the headmaster's quarters, and he began his reign over the school.

Months passed and no one saw the headmaster smile. He didn't smile at staff meetings, of which there were several, for he was a stickler for accountability and a believer in frequent oral reports. He didn't smile when he strolled over the grounds and observed the sweaty boys snaking in front of the tuck shop in a ragged line to buy food or gobbling down a quick bite as they gathered in clumps under the shadow of the old mango tree. And he never smiled at assembly where the boys began the day with the thunder of Methodist hymn singing and the recital of prayers that made the assembly hall rumble as if it was a train passing over a bridge.

The headmaster's wife was his very opposite in disposition. She was a short brown woman with a homely paunch and the genial manner of one who exulted in living. Whenever she encountered the familiar face of a boy, she greeted him like her own long lost sheep. After meeting the same boy three times she invariably remembered his Christian name. When a boarding boy was sick, she would hurry to his bedside and cluck with grandmotherly care over him, sometimes sitting up with a feverish boy deep into the night.

The headmaster and his wife had two daughters, both of whom were plain if not outright ugly. Since Cornwall was a boys' school and bubbling over with thwarted sexual eruptions, the daughters, who were under strict orders not to roam the grounds unnecessarily, confined their airings mainly to the patio in the rear of the headmaster's residence where there was nothing for flesh to provoke but swarms of flies.

One day the stove in the kitchen of the headmaster's quarters ran out of propane and there was no hot food available for lunch. The elder daughter craved a patty and headed for the tuck shop. On the way, she passed the classroom of form 4-B where she was greeted by a wolf whistle from a window. She turned to give a scowling look but saw no one there.

The boys gobbled down lunch, and made their way lethargically back to their classrooms for the arithmetic period and were settling down in a postprandial stupor when the headmaster materialized in the doorway of 4-B, wearing an expression that might have been dug out of a quarry. His mouth line was so sternly compressed that it had become a squiggle. The arithmetic tutor looked inquiringly at the headmaster, who was carrying his flogging cane.

"Excuse me," said the headmaster thinly, "but some boy in this class whistled at my daughter."

"Who among you whistled at the headmaster's daughter?" asked the tutor indignantly, scanning the boys, who were now standing nervously beside their desks.

Everyone knew who had done it, but no one spoke up. All stood as mute and as still as signposts, and every now and again a startlingly bright-red tongue flickered nervously out of a mouth to moisten lips dried by tension.

The headmaster raked the rows of silent boys with his stare.

Finally he said crisply, "Then all must pay if no one is man enough to own up to his crime. Hold out your right hands, palms up."

The boys thrust out their right hands, and the headmaster walked from one boy to the next, slashing each open palm with two strokes of his flogging cane. Since there were thirty boys in the classroom, the punishment took time and effort, and by the time he reached the last boy, the headmaster was visibly breathless.

A few of the boys had tears in their eyes, but none cried openly. One or two rubbed the ugly red welts the stroke of the cane had cut when the blow had missed the open palm and hit the soft flesh of their forearms.

When he was done, the headmaster grimly surveyed the boys, still standing meekly beside their desks, fastening his gaze malignantly on one particular boy, an habitual troublemaker named Maxwell, who stood in the back row scowling darkly.

"Cornwall boys do not behave like hooligans," the headmaster snapped. With one final angry glower, he turned on his heels and marched out of the room.

The boys sat down as one, and the arithmetic tutor began the lesson.

Thirty years passed like a bullet. The boys grew older. The headmaster, having served in that post the longest of any before him, retired and moved into a concrete house in the hills of Montego Bay. His ugly daughters both married German soldiers and presented the headmaster with white grandchildren whose pictures he displayed as ostentatiously as possible and drew to the attention of every visitor.

For a man whose life had been strict and joyless, and whose smile had been so rare that no one had ever glimpsed his teeth, the headmaster had a surprising number of visitors, mainly old boys, most of whom now lived abroad and made annual pilgrimages to the land of their birth and childhood.

With aging came nostalgia, which swept over the old boys like a contagious disease. Suddenly all the unbearable cruelties they had had to endure, preserved in memory and now suffered only in recollection, had become fodder for storytelling and nostalgia. At reunions the boys told and retold stories of the headmaster that bordered on hagiography. A punishment that had once been resented as unnecessarily brutal and wicked, seemed in recollection to have been a healthy part of a stern regimen that had forged them into men. So the boys kept appearing on the doorstep of the headmaster, sometimes in trickles, sometimes in spurts, and almost every one of them was reverential and gentle with the old fellow.

One boy was not.

He remembered the hangman's stare the headmaster used to inflict on the boys at assembly, and he remembered vividly, without the lie of nostalgia and aging, the cruelties the smileless man had committed. He particularly remembered the day the headmaster had beaten an entire class because one myopic boy had whistled at his gruesome daughter. And he meant on his visit to confront the old tyrant with his past iniquities.

He appeared one afternoon at the headmaster's residence and knocked on the gate for at least five minutes before a face timidly peeped through the curtained window. After the loud unbolting of several locks and chains, the back door finally cracked open and two old people peered out at the visitor through a protective steel grill.

The headmaster's wife immediately recognized the middle-aged face framed by the bars of the locked gate and limped down the steps leading from the kitchen to meet the old boy on the concrete driveway and give him a warm, welcoming hug.

"It's Clark," she shouted at the headmaster. "He's come to visit us."

"Clark?" the headmaster repeated feebly from behind a burglar-barred window. "Oh, yes, Clark."

"Sorry we kept you waiting, Clark," the headmaster's wife said mournfully. "But there are thieves and gunmen all over these hills. We live imprisoned in this house."

Clark was soon settled in the drawing room, sipping a glass of home-made lemonade and facing his old tormentor.

"What form were you in again?" the headmaster asked the boy.

"Clark went through all the forms, Eustace," the headmaster's wife interjected briskly. "He began in first form and did Higher Schools in sixth form."

The headmaster replied with a vague, "Oh" and fished out framed photographs of his white grandchildren to show the visiting old boy, who himself was brown, lighter than the headmaster but darker than the grandchildren.

Next the headmaster rambled over snippets of his poor rural childhood and the hard work it took for him to win his degree from Oxford. As he related a tangled tale of how he had won admittance to that august institution by competitive scholarship, the old boy imagined the ridiculous properness such a feat must have required in those days – proper grammar, proper posture, proper attire, proper manners before the examination committee, which would have been made up of cavilling Englishmen looking down their noses at Jamaican applicants. The old boy understood what pressures had squashed the headmaster's mouth and turned it into an ink-drawn line.

But in spite of these intimacies, what he found galling was that the tyrant seemed to remember none of his particular iniquities, indeed did not even think of himself as ever having been the incarnation of capricious wickedness.

"Do you remember the day", the old boy probed in a tone of faked geniality as he dutifully leafed through the photo album of white grandchildren, "when you caned all of 4-B because someone in it had whistled at your daughter?"

The headmaster looked up from his muttered annotations of the photos and said, "No, I don't remember. I wouldn't have done that. It's not like me."

"It was just like you!" the old boy snapped.

"Every old boy who visits brings a different scrap of memory with him," the headmaster's wife said serenely. "If we could lay all the scraps side by side, we'd have the whole picture."

"I don't remember half of what the boys tell me happened," the headmaster said in a voice faint with the confusion and tremulousness of age.

"Well, I remember everything", the old boy said disagreeably.

"The important thing", chirped the headmaster's wife, "is that we've all come through those difficult years and have now reached higher ground."

The headmaster excused himself and shuffled off to the bathroom. In his absence, his wife poured more lemonade and made small talk. She was discussing her hobby of growing begonias when the old boy interrupted.

"He's been gone a long time, hasn't he?" he said, shooting a glance at the mouth of the hallway that had swallowed up the headmaster.

"Old bowels don't work as well as they used to," the headmaster's wife replied serenely. "Old minds forget. Old hearts forgive."

"Not all old hearts," the old boy contradicted.

The headmaster's wife took a deep breath, threw a furtive glance over her shoulder at the hallway, and whispered, "I know Eustace was harsh with you boys. But if you want people to follow you through the jungle of Jamaica, you have to leave visible footsteps."

A toilet flushed and the headmaster returned to the drawing room to sink into a soft chair that practically engulfed his frail body like a giant amoeba.

"Did I ever tell you, Maxwell, about the time ...?" the headmaster began.

"This is Clark, dear," his wife interrupted gently. "Maxwell was here last month."

"Oh, yes," said the headmaster listlessly. "Clark."

"It was Maxwell who whistled at your daughter," the old boy muttered spitefully.

The headmaster peered across the room as if the old boy was smothered in a fog bank.

"You keep saying that someone whistled at my daughter," he remarked. "But I just don't remember any such incident."

"Maxwell is now a respected orthopaedic surgeon in Washington, DC," his wife said. "More lemonade, Clark?"

"Did you know, Maxwell, that I was the first coloured Jamaican boy admitted to Oxford from Westmoreland?"

"Yes, dear, Clark and Maxwell both know. And they're very proud of you."

"Thank you," the headmaster said, looking bemused. "I can tell you it wasn't easy."

The old boy departed a few minutes later, the headmaster's wife sending him off with a knowing hug, the headmaster walking him to the gate and giving him a wrinkled hand of aging gristle to squeeze.

After watching the headmaster hobble back up the driveway and disappear inside his fortified residence to the unmusical clunking of deadbolts, the old boy climbed into his car feeling like a man who, finally given the chance to scratch an itchy spot that had tormented him for years, finds that he has no fingernails.

He drove slowly down the winding road that tumbled past concrete homes whose windows wore eye-patches of burglar bars and whose open doorways bared steel grills at the world, and past the grounds of Cornwall College.

The ancient gate of the school, hanging ajar on its hinges like an open mouth, was drooling rambunctious boys into the street who dribbled in beads of khaki down the steep hillside. It seemed that only yesterday, he had been one of those lower-form boys in short pants. Now he was that classic oxymoron, an old boy.

In his imagination, he vividly glimpsed a slide-show of scenes from the headmaster's life: his humble rural beginnings, his late-night swatting of school books, his fussing with deportment and appearance, his struggles to speak the King's English instead of the guttural Jamaican patois and, finally, his lifelong modelling of this patchwork effigy of colonial propriety before hundreds of Jamaican boys stewing in the hormones of adolescence.

He drove slowly towards the tangled heart of downtown Montego Bay. Stuck in the back of his mind was yet another episode of wickedness that he had meant to bring to the old tyrant's attention. Only last week he had been reliving it in all its horror. What was it again? It would soon come back to him.

And damn it to hell, he still did not forgive.

The Happy Days of Dog Eat Dog

PETER Smith of Smith and Smith was a prosperous solicitor at a long established legal practice in Kingston. The practice had been started by his paternal grandfather in 1892, inherited by his father, and was intended to be passed on to successive generations of Smiths. Even though he was only a junior partner, Peter made a lot of money from it, and he lived very well on his income. He met and married an American tourist, Marilyn, who was vacationing in Jamaica, had children, and built a house so high up on a mountain top in Beverly Hills that from its tiled, spacious veranda even nasty, thuggish Kingston appeared at night as innocent and glittery as a Christmas tree.

With the passing of his father, Peter was elevated to senior partner and his income, already considerable, quadrupled, enabling him to build a vacation cottage in a posh resort community on the North Coast.

His cottage was a cottage in name only. In fact it was a substantial four-bedroom, four-bathroom house with a pool and servants' quarters, but the conceit of this particular resort was to make every villa owner feel like a boy by calling their house a *cottage*, a misnomer maliciously begun by an English resident manager to discourage villa owners from acting too uppity.

To look after his bogus cottage, Peter hired a young man named Sylvester Burke to act as general overseer and handyman. As part of his wages, Sylvester was given a room in the servants' quarters of the house, where he lived alone with an occasional visit from whatever girlfriend happened to be current in his life.

Everything went well for ten years under this arrangement. Sylvester stayed at the cottage, with Peter and his family coming down mainly on weekends and for the odd week or two during the summer holidays. The rest of the time the house was either vacant or rented to tourists. It was a solid concrete structure, and its yard required little maintenance, since it was mainly landscaped with rugged bushes and shrubs that grew naturally in the parish. Mowing and watering the scrap of lawn in the front yard next to the swimming pool was the only upkeep required.

During the election season of 1976, Sylvester began to get restless. He became bad-tempered with the cook, who was full-time when guests were renting the cottage and, when they were not, came in once a week to sweep up and dust. The conflict between him and the cook became so ugly and occasioned so many bitter phone calls between the cottage and Kingston that Peter was forced to intervene. He drove down to the house one Saturday by himself, meaning to settle once and for all the trouble between his two employees, even if it meant firing one or the other.

On his arrival, he summoned Sylvester and the cook to a meeting and demanded to know what was wrong. Sylvester took on an apologetic tone and admitted that most of the trouble between him and the cook was his fault because he was so unhappy in his present situation.

When guests were not present and the house was clean, he said, there was little else to do but water the lawn. However, with the election campaign raging, the political bloodletting had given Jamaica a bad name abroad, severely reducing the number of overseas bookings. The result was that with only the lawn to take care of he had become bored.

"It don't say nothing, boss," Sylvester complained about the lawn. "Every day it just sit here waiting for my watering. Day in and day out, me one out in dis little yard giving it water. How much longer can dis go on? Me is not a boy of sixteen again. Me's a man of twenty-six. Me need motion."

A sympathetic Peter saw that without tourist bookings, there really was little work for Sylvester to do. It was not the chap's fault that the socialists were making a shambles of Jamaica with their constant harping on the unfair divide between the classes, sparking a mass exodus of Jamaicans for England and the US. And although Peter abhorred socialism, he was realistic enough to grasp that in Jamaica the vast differences between the haves and the have-nots made its appeals attractive to a certain mentality.

What was needed to answer socialism, in his opinion, was enlightened leadership from the ruling class, of which he was a chartered member, and he set his sights on solving Sylvester's problem in order to demonstrate the good that such leadership could quietly accomplish.

After the cook had departed, Peter invited the handyman to sit on his veranda, to cock up foot and to speak his heart's ambition. A few beers later, Sylvester admitted that what he really wanted to do was to operate an all-island taxi. Such a job would allow him the freedom to travel all over Jamaica and give him contact with a wide variety of different people, every one of whom would surely have a brighter personality than the dowdy lawn. He could continue to live at the house and, when the tourists returned, he could offer them pick-up and drop-off at the Montego Bay airport.

His difficulty was that he couldn't get a driver's licence because the local examination depot was desperately understaffed and backed up for months. There was no point in even showing up in the hope that he might be examined. Sylvester had already done that three or four times only to be turned away at the end of the day without being tested. He had registered on a waiting list, but the examination office had sent him back a form letter saying that no appointments were being made at this time. However, if conditions should improve, he would be notified. It was a typical bureaucratic dodge of responsibility by an incompetent socialist government.

"There's a way out of this," said Peter magnanimously. "I'll fix it for you in a week or so."

"Thank you, sah," Sylvester replied gratefully. Then, after a polite pause to allow his gratitude to sink in, he asked dubiously, "How, sah?"

"The way things have been fixed in Jamaica since the beginning of time," Peter said confidently. "With a bribe."

"A bribe? Who you going bribe, sah?"

"One of the examiners, of course," Peter said bluntly.

Sylvester chuckled with delight at the idea of his employer, a big-time Kingston solicitor, bribing a country bumpkin motor-vehicle examiner.

"Bribery is the Jamaican way," Peter said expansively. "As long as we Jamaicans can bribe one another, we'll be all right. It'll continue to be dog eat dog, every man for himself. If we ever reach the stage where it's no longer dog eat dog, watch out! That's when the ideologues will take over and the country will be in deep trouble."

Sylvester barely understood what his employer was saying but was too proud to ask for clarification, so he merely nodded sagely and croaked, "True, sah," bobbing his head like a strutting hen that had just laid an egg.

"Now take this evening," Peter boasted. "Two Jamaicans from different classes, one high, so-called, and one low, so-called, yet we can still sit down and drink a beer and enjoy camaraderie. The politicians hate that."

"You is high, sah, and me is low?" Sylvester asked politely.

"Yes, according to Mr Manley and the socialists."

A ticklish silence descended over the veranda. It was as if the raw nerves of a decaying tooth had suddenly become exposed to the night air.

"Want another beer, Sylvester?" Peter asked soothingly.

"Yes, sah, thank you," Sylvester replied, reaching for one. And with the additional infusion of alcohol, the ticklish moment quickly passed.

The remainder of the night both men got drunk and seemed to thoroughly enjoy each other's company in spite of their social differences. Peter held forth on politics, using many big words that Sylvester did not fully understand but which he deeply appreciated, for they reflected well on him by confirming that his employer was truly a learned man and not a Butu. Every time Peter used another big word, Sylvester inhaled deeply as if to savour its aroma.

At around three in the morning, Peter staggered off to his bed in the master suite and Sylvester fumbled his way down to the back room of the servants' quarters.

Peter returned to Kingston the next day, and although Sylvester was fretful that he would forget his promise to help him get a driver's licence, the solicitor began work on the problem the first day back in office. Using the authority of Smith and Smith, he sought out the ubiquitous problem-solver on the island: the friend of a friend. And eventually he found such a person who knew someone who knew someone in the Trelawny motor vehicle examination department who, if his palms were properly greased, would accelerate the testing process for Sylvester.

The political climate, meanwhile, had degenerated from bad to worse. There were shootings almost every day and spontaneous roadblocks in the streets. Normally confined to the ghettos, the violence spilled out across Kingston and erupted randomly around some of the better residential neighbourhoods. A prominent resident of St Andrew was murdered in an inexplicable episode for he was known to have apolitical views and, for all anyone could tell, hadn't an enemy in the world. Everywhere across the land people were uprooting themselves from substantial homes and fleeing the island.

One evening Peter and Marilyn were sitting on their veranda, having a last drink with the couple next door who had decided to leave Jamaica for good. The couple had the usual reasons – they were frightened of the violence and the random murders, Jamaica was just not the same as it used to be, they were thinking of their children, now was the time to go before the government turned communist and took away all their personal possessions, etc., etc., etc.

After the final goodbyes, Marilyn and Peter lingered on the veranda, talking.

"Do you think we should move to America?" Marilyn asked hopefully. "Daddy said he'd make you a partner once you passed the bar."

Peter grumped that he didn't think it was time to leave yet, that Jamaica was still the same as it had always been, and to prove his point he drunkenly told the story about how he intended to bribe a motor-vehicle examiner to test Sylvester. Marilyn had some reservations about any kind of bribery, but Peter assured her that what he was doing was a time-honoured Jamaican practice. He went on to argue that bribery was a kind of natural protection against socialism and ideology.

"How can that be?" Marilyn wondered.

Peter explained his theory of why a dog-eat-dog lifestyle was good for the country, why the every-man-for-himself ethic was a hedge against socialism and any other ideology.

"You're drunk," Marilyn yawned and went to bed.

Peter fell asleep on the veranda, woke up about four in the morning and shambled off to join her.

As he stumbled towards his bedroom, he exulted in the fact that he had fallen asleep on his veranda and not been murdered. He almost woke up Marilyn to show her how un-murdered he was, and how this only went to prove that Jamaica was the same as it had ever been, and that people were worried about nothing.

The bribery meeting being arranged, Peter drove over to the North Coast, picked up Sylvester, and together they travelled to the test facility in Falmouth.

The examiner turned out to be a surprisingly young man with a chip on his shoulder and a swaggering attitude. Even though he knew that Peter and Sylvester were waiting to give him a bribe, he sat at his desk, sullenly immersed in a pile of papers on which he energetically scribbled whenever either man made eye contact with him.

Eventually, after the young man was satisfied with his display of authority, he got up nonchalantly from his chair and sauntered over to them. Peter stood up to greet him.

"Follow me," the examiner said curtly.

Sylvester jumped to his feet, too.

"Not you," the man said. "You," and he pointed to Peter.

He led him through a warren of hallways to a shabby, unfurnished room in the back of the building. Every breath Peter drew stank of mould.

The examiner turned to face him. "You have dat thing?" he asked Peter.

Peter handed him a brown envelope. The examiner opened it and did a quick count of the money before folding the envelope in half and tucking it into his pocket.

"Just a minute," Peter asked as the man was about to duck through the door. "This means he'll pass, right?"

"No, it doesn't," the examiner said coolly. "It means he'll be tested. He must pass on his own."

"That's not the way I understand our arrangement. My friend of your friend told me this would guarantee a pass."

"Only de applicant's skills behind de wheel can do dat, sah."

"He passes or my money back," Peter said, placing a restraining hand on the examiner's arm, causing the man to stiffen.

"If you say so," the examiner replied thinly. "Bring de vehicle around to de front."

Then he was gone down the hallway, towards the waiting room, where Sylvester, along with a rag-tag crowd of other applicants, sat patiently waiting in the heat.

"Listen," Peter whispered to Sylvester, "this is a serious man. Drive as carefully as you can for him."

"Yes, sah," Sylvester said nervously.

Peter brought the car around. The examiner got in the front passenger seat, Sylvester got behind the wheel, and the car drove off with a nervous lurch.

Thirty minutes later the car returned to the curb where Peter was still pacing. Sylvester had failed the examination. The examiner handed him an official sheet with his flunking score scribbled in its top margin.

"Come wid me," he said to Peter and they retreated to the same back room that stank of mould where the brown envelope changed hands again. Peter looked at the envelope with an expression of consternation.

"But what kind of thing is this?" Peter wailed. "You took my money and now you giving it back?"

"The money was for giving him de examination. But he must be able to pass on his own. Now, I have other people waiting. You know you way out or you want to follow me?"

"I'll follow," Peter mumbled, and the man set off at a brisk clip.

They were ploughing through the smelly government hallway when a conviction struck Peter smack in the face.

"You're a socialist, aren't you?"

The examiner cut him with a scornful glance.

"I'm a man of principle," he replied coolly.

"That's the problem with Jamaica today," Peter grumbled. "Too much damn ideology."

"Bring de applicant back when he knows how to drive," the examiner snapped.

On the way back to the cottage Peter handed the thousand dollars to Sylvester and advised him to find an unprincipled examiner to bribe who was not a socialist.

Returning to Kingston, Peter announced to his wife that he had made a decision. The socialists were everywhere, and their alien ideology was spreading all over Jamaica. He was now convinced that the happy days of dog eat dog were numbered. It was time for them to migrate to America.

"If you say so, dear," she said demurely, her heart racing with joy.

Three months later the Smiths sold out lock, stock and barrel and moved to Connecticut.

Sylvester, meanwhile, after some difficulty found another examiner who was open to a bribe, but not a monetary one. What the man wanted badly was to have sex with a certain woman in the parish who had once been one of Sylvester's girlfriends. Sylvester coaxed her into doing it, secretly paying her five hundred dollars, and the day afterwards he received his driver's licence without even taking the test.

He pocketed the remaining five hundred dollars.

The Annihilation of Fish

FISH was a fighter of the Devil. He didn't fight the Devil every day, or every week or even every month. It wasn't a regularly scheduled fight. Fish never really knew when the Devil might appear ready for a fight, although he usually had a vague idea that something was building up and would begin training in preparation for it. He trained by jogging down Hollywood Boulevard in the early morning, by doing noisy knee-bends against the peeling walls of his dim apartment, and by eating raw spinach and fried garbonza beans. He would notify Poinsettia, his referee, that a fight was coming up. After that, they would wait for the Devil.

When Fish had lived in New York, he had never had a referee. He fought the Devil in private, with no witnesses. But that was before the subway fight.

In that fight, the Devil had sneaked up on Fish in a crowded subway car, and they had locked in a furious struggle. Passengers were hurled against each other as Fish gripped the wriggling Devil in a hammerlock and tried to pin him. There was a frantic screaming and shoving. Several passengers panicked and tried to throw themselves out of the window. The train limped into the station and Fish was seized by alerted police officers and carried away, still grappling with the Devil, to a mental institution in Queens. There, Fish was given a choice. He could have a lobotomy or he could agree to (a) never again fight the Devil in a public place, and (b) always have a referee on hand to officiate his private fights with the Devil. Fish declined the lobotomy and signed an affidavit agreeing to the latter terms. Shortly afterwards he moved to Hollywood and met Poinsettia, who became his referee.

He met Poinsettia in Mrs Muldroon's apartment building. Poinsettia had just moved to Hollywood from San Francisco and occupied the apartment next to Fish's. They shared a battered rubbish bin at the end of the flaking corridor. Soon, they became friends.

Poinsettia was white, but it made no difference to Fish, who was black, because at seventy-six his eyes were so bad that he saw everything as yellow. The sky was yellow; Hollywood Boulevard was yellow; Poinsettia was yellow.

When Fish met anyone he knew, he immediately told them how nice and yellow they looked. At first, some people were startled by this and would go away and search in the mirror for signs of yellowing, until they got used to Fish. Others always got mad at Fish and angrily denied that they were yellow. Many people avoided him, so they would not have to listen to Fish telling them how yellow they looked.

So it didn't matter to Fish that Poinsettia was yellow, because so was everyone else. It was Poinsettia's vile habits that upset him.

Poinsettia was seventy-four, but she still smoked cigars and cursed. She drank whisky whenever she could afford to buy a bottle on her Social Security cheque. She cheated Fish at gin rummy.

But most of the time, they got along well. They got along so well that Poinsettia kept asking Fish to marry her.

"How's a man going to marry his referee, Poinsettia?" Fish protested in an aggrieved voice. "Whoever heard of such a thing? Plus," he added as Poinsettia glared at him, "I'd be weaken by the marriage bonds and get annihilated 'cause I won't have no strength left to fight with. Marriage's too much work for a fighting man!"

Poinsettia became enraged and stomped out of the small apartment, slamming the door violently behind her. Immediately afterwards, the sound of a doleful aria from *Madam Butterfly* floated down the fraying hallway of the second floor, as Poinsettia closeted herself with Jim Beam and Puccini, and got mournfully drunk. Fish banged on her door and pleaded with her to come out, but she screamed obscenities at him and stayed locked in her room for days, going on a sorrowful binge.

When they were not fighting each other, and when Fish was not in training, they spent long smoggy afternoons together playing gin rummy and keeping each other company. Fish would tell Poinsettia ghost stories which he remembered from his childhood in Jamaica, and Poinsettia would smoke cigars and cheat at gin rummy. And they would both wait for the Devil to show up for his fight with Fish.

Poinsettia did not quite understand why of all the people to choose as an opponent, the Devil had chosen Fish. Sometimes she questioned Fish mildly on this point, but if he seemed taciturn, as he usually did, she would drop the subject. She did not think it *that* unusual that Fish fought with the Devil. After all, she herself had talked with Puccini many times about *Madam Butterfly*. When she lived in San Francisco she had even proposed marriage to Puccini, he was spending so much time at her apartment, and he had accepted. But they were not able to find a minister enlightened enough to marry them. The affair ended shortly afterwards because, much as she swore and drank and smoked cigars, Poinsettia adamantly refused to live with Puccini out of wedlock. No matter how much she loved him and his *Butterfly*, Poinsettia explained to a heartbroken Puccini, she would not be a fallen woman.

They had a tender and heartfelt separation scene, with Puccini weeping bitterly and reaching an outstretched hand to Poinsettia, and Poinsettia covering her face with her fingers and turning her head modestly away from his blandishments. It was like something out of *Butterfly*. And when it was over, Poinsettia moved to Hollywood, where she met Fish and became his referee.

During the past two years, she had refereed thirteen fights between Fish and the Devil, and each time Fish had won.

But secretly Poinsettia wished that Fish would lose and that the Devil would go away and leave them alone. Secretly, too, Poinsettia loathed the Devil. Because of the Devil, Fish would never marry her. He was too afraid of being annihilated. He would never marry his referee.

Poinsettia had become desperate. She was so desperate that after the last fight she had gone out and bought a gun from a pawnshop. She was so desperate that she planned to murder the Devil.

One Saturday morning, just as Poinsettia was getting ready to slip into a hot bath, Fish ran down the flaking hallway and pounded on her door.

"Poinsettia!" he shouted, with urgency. "Get ready! I got a bout coming!"

Poinsettia muttered a curse, put on a dressing gown, slipped the gun into its pocket, grabbed a stick she used to cudgel the Devil if he became obnoxious, and scampered down the hallway into Fish's room.

There she found Fish in the dim living room, his nostrils flaring, his eyes blazing, leaning and rocking in the ready stance of a wrestler. Poinsettia elbowed her way past an overstuffed chair and pushed a linoleum-covered table out of her way.

"All right," she announced grimly, "no gouging, no kicking, no biting and whoever don't obey I'll bust his head open!"

Fish nodded, wet his lips and glared hard at his invisible opponent.

"OK. Ready?" Poinsettia asked, holding her stick aloft.

"Ready!" Fish breathed, his eyes fixed and staring across the room.

"Go!" Poinsettia yelled.

Fish circled, his large black arms outstretched, his hands curling and probing for an opening. He leaped backwards to escape a diving lunge and crashed into a wall. He bounced off the wall and circled some more, his eyes darting around the small room, his body crouched and tense.

Circling and weaving and windmilling his arms, Fish moved through the living room, breathing loudly through his open mouth.

Suddenly, he stiffened. The veins in his neck leaped out into rigid strings; his arms locked around his opponent; he began a jerking, grappling, grunting dance around the small living room. He rocked back and forth, his arms fastened around the Devil's neck. He swayed backwards as the Devil made a tremendous push, then crashed heavily on the floor, squirming, kicking and grunting. Poinsettia circled, staring down as Fish twisted and squirmed on the floor, trying to brace himself against the wall to throw off the Devil.

With a loud groan, Fish wriggled a quivering leg under the Devil and pushed him off. Then he leaped at him, fell on his belly and rolled over and over, wriggling and squirming against the wall.

"Foul blow! Foul blow!" Poinsettia shouted, rushing over to where a grunting, twisting Fish lay pinned against the wall. She flailed the air with the stick and reached down to pull the wriggling Devil off Fish.

Fish went limp, and glared upwards. He clambered shakily to his feet.

"He almost had me, Poinsettia," Fish gasped, blinking and regaining his balance. "I's sure glad you saw the way he was holding me."

"I told you once, we don't allow no below the belt holding," Poinsettia rasped at the Devil.

Fish was panting and sweating in the small room. The beads of sweat glinted off his shiny black face, his mouth was open, and he was breathing with a laboured wheeze.

"One minute break," the referee snapped. "One minute!"

"He says he don't wanna break," Fish gasped, trying to catch his breath.

"Tell the so and so I'm the referee around here," Poinsettia snarled, wielding the stick over her head. "When I say break, we break!"

"He don't like it," Fish breathed heavily, sitting down on the floor. He wrapped his arms over his knees and hung his head against his chest as he struggled to breathe.

"You OK, Fish?" Poinsettia stood over him and rested a hand on his shoulder.

"He objects that you's a partial referee," Fish gasped peevishly, pushing her hand away.

"Where's he now?" Poinsettia asked, her eyes darting rapidly around the small room. "Where's he exactly?"

"See that chair over dere?" Fish gestured towards a wooden chair over in the far corner. "He's sitting on it."

"He still there?" Poinsettia turned and stared intently at the chair.

"Yeah," Fish nodded, "He there."

Poinsettia ambled casually over to the chair. She stood beside it, staring. "He still there?" she asked nonchalantly.

"Yeah!" Fish gasped again, beginning to make a noisy wheeze.

Poinsettia whipped out the gun and fired at the chair at point-blank range. The gunshot cracked through the dark hallways of the brick building. Fish leaped to his feet with horror and disbelief.

"Poinsettia!" he gasped, putting a large hand to his mouth in a gesture of incredulity. "What you done?"

"Did I get him? Did I get him? Did I get him?" Poinsettia asked excitedly.

"You's blown his head open," Fish managed to say, stumbling over to the chair in a daze and staring at the floor.

"I got him!" Poinsettia exclaimed loudly. Then she jumped wildly up and down waving the stick in one hand and the pistol in the other, and screamed with joy, "I got him! I got him! I got him!"

Fish was kneeling on the floor, rubbing his hand over the frayed carpet. He turned his palm upwards and stared at it with shock on his face.

"He's bleeding bad, Poinsettia," Fish stammered. "You shouldn't have done that. You shot him in the head."

Poinsettia levelled the gun for a *coup de grâce* shot at the spot from which Fish had just removed his hand, but before she could fire, he jumped up, wrestled the gun away from her and threw it clattering on the table. They stood glowering at each other.

"This is the worst thing you ever done," Fish said angrily. "Foul play! You done involved me in foul play!"

"Poinsettia! Fish!" Mrs Muldroon's voice drifted up from the landing below.

Chuckling triumphantly, Poinsettia walked to the door and opened it.

"We're here, Mrs Muldroon," she bawled.

"Was that a shot I heard?" Mrs Muldroon asked anxiously.

"It sure as hell was," Poinsettia roared back. "I plugged Fish's Devil in his head."

Silence drifted up from the landing as Mrs Muldroon thought this over. "Well," she called back, "I hope you don't get bloodstains on the carpet. I can't afford a new carpet just now."

"Don't worry, Mrs Muldroon," Poinsettia shouted back, madness gleaming in her eyes. "We'll clean it up. You won't notice a thing."

Another thread of silence floated up from the landing and through the peeling hallway. Then the sound of a small scraping retreat drifted up as Mrs Muldroon picked her way back to her apartment.

"OK," a faint and hesitant reply came back. "So long as you clean up the mess, I don't care who you shoot."

Poinsettia shut the door and came back into the dim living room. Fish was on his knees, rubbing his hands above the carpet as if massaging a wound.

"What're you doing?" Poinsettia asked gruffly, staring down at him.

"I'm trying to give him first aid," Fish said over his shoulder, pressing down as if on a body. "He's going fast on me."

"Serves him right," Poinsettia snapped irreverently. She tried to angle past the kneeling Fish so she could help the moribund Devil along with a kick.

"This is like Mrs Mohammed Ali shooting Joe Fraser in the ring," Fish said sorrowfully, rubbing both hands above the carpet and pressing down. "I been annihilated."

"The hell you say," Poinsettia roared angrily, her brow clustering together in a dark frown.

"I been annihilated, woman," Fish moaned. "You don't understand. I lost by default."

"You dummy!" Poinsettia fumed. "You haven't been annihilated! I shot him."

"Yeah," Fish said in a low voice, "but you done it for me. Therefore I's now annihilated. I beat him all these years by meself, now you done plugged him and annihilated me."

"Jesus Christ!" Poinsettia stormed, rushing into the kitchen. She ran into the living room brandishing a bread knife. "I'm going to finish him off."

"It's too late," Fish said sadly, standing with his head bowed. "He just passed on."

"He's dead?" Poinsettia gulped, staring wild-eyed at the empty, fraying carpet.

"You blows his head off," Fish said disconsolately, looking down at his feet with listless sorrow.

Poinsettia broke into a hysterical, profane laughter, her eyes flashing with triumph. Seeing the look of inconsolable sadness on Fish's face, however, she put the bread knife down on the linoleum-covered table and walked over to stand beside him.

"You done a bad thing, Poinsettia," Fish said softly, looking at his feet and bowing his head in grief.

"I did it for you, Fish," Poinsettia laid a comforting hand on the old black man's shoulders.

He shrugged it off with finality and walked over and stood by the window with his back to her. Off Hollywood Boulevard the whine of morning noises moaned through the room like the cries of a lost insect.

Poinsettia stared down at the frayed carpet where the dead Devil was supposed to be. She pushed at a frayed tuft with a tentative toe, as if warily turning over the body of a fallen enemy. She gave it a sly, final kick.

Fish's shoulders slumped forwards and began to jerk spasmodically. He crumpled against the window and began to cry.

"Fish!" Poinsettia was quickly at his side and trying to turn him around. "Fish!" she begged.

Fish hung his head and tried to shake her away.

"Fish!" Poinsettia pleaded. "For God's sake, Fish!"

"I been annihilated," Fish howled, bent over and sobbing at the window. "You annihilated me, Poinsettia. Now I's a beaten man."

"For Christ's sake, Fish!" Poinsettia snapped, trying to turn him around to face her.

But Fish would not turn. He burrowed against the window and sobbed, his breath frosting the pane in mournful, uneven, grey smudges. Poinsettia pocketed the murder weapon and slipped guiltily out of the room.

There was a funeral in the small patch of yard behind Mrs Muldroon's red-brick apartment building. Years before, when Mr Muldroon was alive, he planted turnips and carrots in the small patch of yard, but after he died of bowel cancer it was abandoned to dandelions and chickweed. Now, with Mrs Muldroon's permission, Fish dug a cavernous grave in the small yard. It took him two long days to do it. After he had spaded out only a shallow two inches of dirt from the flinty ground, he almost abandoned the idea of burying the Devil, except that Mrs Muldroon roused him from a semi-stupored brooding by pounding on his door and complaining angrily about the smell from the decomposing demon.

"It don't smell bad to me," Fish had declared through the closed door, his voice drawling in an unaccustomed sadness.

"It smells to me," Mrs Muldroon snapped back. "If you won't bury it, I'll call the Health Department."

Fish was therefore forced to resume digging the grave for the murdered Devil.

When the grave was dug, he marched lugubriously down the dark corridor, carrying the body wrapped in an American flag. Fish tromped solemnly through the peeling hallways, down the creaking wooden staircase, past Mrs Muldroon's apartment and out into the small yard. He was joined at the graveside by Mrs Muldroon, who squinted painfully in the bright sunlight.

Fish stood gauntly over the grave, a small wetness in the corners of his eyes, and mumbled the funeral service in a whispered voice.

"At least", Mrs Muldroon consoled him, patting the bowed-over Fish on the shoulder, "he lived a full life, and a long one. What more can you ask for?"

"Done in by foul play," Fish muttered, staring into the grave. "And now I's annihilated."

"I'm certain Poinsettia meant well," Mrs Muldroon said firmly.

"But she done bad," Fish whispered. "She done mighty bad."

Torn by grief, he refused to say anything more.

Meanwhile, Poinsettia had gone on a four-day drunk. The smell of sour cigar smoke haunted the long, fraying corridor she shared with Fish. Aria after aria by Puccini squealed through the dark stairwell of the red-brick building.

Inside, Poinsettia sat in a threadbare blue chair and drank whisky, smoked cigars and lived on cans of alphabet soup. Sometimes she sobbed wildly to herself in the small apartment. Sometimes she paced restlessly and cursed Fish in a slurred, thick monotone.

She walked to the window of her small apartment and looked down over dark alleys and tarpaper roofs at the neon glitter of Hollywood Boulevard and was overwhelmed by a sense of her loss.

Once she staggered down the frayed corridor and banged loudly on Fish's door. She stood before the implacable door, knocking and crying for Fish to come out and talk to her. Inside, Fish hid himself under the bed and covered his ears with his hands.

After pounding on the door for twenty futile minutes, Poinsettia was finally driven off by Mrs Muldroon. Poinsettia lurched back into her own empty apartment and drank herself into another stupor.

For the next two weeks, Fish wandered lethargically down Hollywood Boulevard. He stayed in his room during the days, venturing out listlessly at night to trudge past flickering shop windows and elbow his way through throngs of street people.

He became inconsolable. He began to lose weight. His cheeks shrank. He took on a gaunt, weary look. One morning he woke up with a raging fever. Two days later, he developed pneumonia. At almost the same time, Poinsettia mysteriously disappeared.

Fish lay on his sickbed over the next few days. Mrs Muldroon, her joints frozen by spasms of arthritis, came to his room every day and sat with him. She fed him beef broth and milk and strained vegetables. She forced him to take antibiotics and aspirin and told him stories about her late husband and how it was with them when they were young together in Iowa.

Fish slipped into a delirious sleep. His limbs trembled and shook under the blankets. He called out for dead relatives in the Jamaican dialect. When he was awake, he stared at the window with a blank, expressionless grief in his eyes, his black brow glinting with sweat from the fever.

On the fourth day of his sickness, there was a timid knock on the door. Mrs Muldroon answered it, and Poinsettia stepped into the room.

Poinsettia, too, had changed. She had lost weight. There were blue shadows of sleeplessness under her eyes. Her hands shook with the DT's. She smelled of cigar smoke and sour sweat.

She came hesitantly into the room, holding her right hand out, as if she was leading someone behind her. In her left hand, she carried a worn, beaded bag.

"Fish," Poinsettia began, blinking furiously and drawing near his bed, "Fish, ... Please, Fish, look at me."

Fish turned his head away and looked towards the window.

"Fish," Poinsettia yelled, tears streaming down her yellow face. "Look at me!"

Fish turned wearily and looked up at her. Mrs Muldroon circled tactfully out of sight and sat in a nearby chair, her head slumping on her chest.

"This is Puccini, Fish," Poinsettia gestured to the invisible figure clinging to her right hand.

Fish stared up at her, blinking with feverish incomprehension.

"How do ye do," he muttered, self-consciously pulling the blanket up to his neck in the presence of a stranger.

"I went to San Francisco by bus to get him," Poinsettia said, waving at Puccini with a helpless, fatalistic gesture. "I wanted you to see this, Fish," she choked.

Suddenly, she pushed the unsuspecting Puccini away and pulled the gun out of the beaded handbag.

Puccini yelped with horror and ran for the door, but it was too late. Poinsettia fired three times, hitting him in the back. Then she dropped the gun and burst into a wild, hysterical sobbing.

"Poinsettia!" Fish cried weakly from his bed.

"I used to love him, Fish," Poinsettia sobbed in anguish beside the bed, "but I love you more! I love you more!"

With that, she crumpled into the outstretched arms of Fish and, crying hysterically, she hugged him on the wobbling bed.

Gurgles of love filled the room as Mrs Muldroon, her face flushed with bewilderment, glowered suspiciously at the spot where the bullet-riddled body of the betrayed Puccini had fallen, and muttered crossly, "He better not bleed on my carpet."